I Was Warned Not To Publish This Book Is The Word Processor Mightier Than The H-Bomb?

An Open Letter To President Biden And Other Essays?

Maurice G. Faucette

I was Warned Not to Publish this Book!

Dedication

I dedicate the book to my mother, Dorothy Mae Mosley Faucette, from Atmore, Alabama. How she worked so hard to raise her children, I do not know. I saw her go with little sleep at times..

She pushed us to get an education. How she stood up to the powers that be, I do not know. Her Grand Children and Great Grand's have and are attending the best schools in America. I got the attitude of being outspoken and sometimes not giving a GD from her.

May God Bless and Keep her. I always told the kids I coached to make their mothers proud.

Ma, I trust I make you proud!

Table of Contents

Foreword

The title of Maurice Faucette's book is aptly named and is a good read for those who are not only seeking knowledge but also truth. Mr. Faucette has the receipts and knows the facts, because he was there. Many of the Power Brokers fear a man of his knowledge, wisdom, honesty, integrity, and intellect because, as they say in the streets, "he knows where the bodies are buried."

More than his formal education, which includes a Finance Degree from North Carolina Central University, where he served as the Keynote Speaker at homecoming, and attended the Masters Degree in Business Administration program at Fordham University. He also holds a PhD. D. from UCLA, "Upon the Corner of Lenox Avenue", where he was raised on 115th Street in South Harlem. Like the Honorable Elijah Muhammad, Minister Malcolm X, and the Honorable Louis Farrakhan, he comes from a Liberation Theology background and believes, "The Black man will never be respected until he learns to do for self!" So, naturally, he was warned by the "Buffer Class," the Black Elite, not to write this book because they subscribe to the Black Misleadership of depending on a system of free that leaves them dependent on the system, maintaining the status quo.

Maurice Faucette is an asset to the Harlem Community. He founded the South Harlem Reds Baseball team and has been a godsend to many single mothers. Many of the kids he coached received scholarships for higher education, but most importantly, he became a surrogate father, leading them to Manhood through sportsmanship, teamwork, and focus, which assisted them in their academic studies. They also learned from him financial literacy, customer service, and marketing skills, as Maurice was a leader in the Corporate Sector. He has the ability to connect with an audience better than most preachers, making him a great motivational speaker. Again, he was warned not to write this book because this is what most people fear Maurice Faucette, a child from 115th in Harlem, is the Truth.

Mark McPhee was features writer for the Fahari Newspaper and the Deuce Club Newsletter distributed in the New York State Prison System. He is also a member of Harlem Liberation School, Harlem Emergency Network, Associate Producer on the Sistah Talk Radio Show hosted by Dietra Kelsey and former contributor on WHCR 90.3 Harlem 411 Radio Show and the Circle of Brothers.

Preface

I have always written essays and commentary. While working at Xerox Corporation, communication through the sky came into effect through Ethernet and the Internet. Black Professionals working for Xerox set up a group called the Black Network.

Finding time away from their jobs, the group shared information and discussed and debated topics. I wrote prolifically on the network. In fact, I was consumed with it. I spent too many hours during the day and stayed late at night. Most of what we discussed was not work-related. It was about the Black Experience. It was about the good, the bad and the ugly.

Through the Black network, I met two Brothers, Robert Bain and Gerald Brown. We became the "Stars" of the Black Network. Our debates became legendary. In fact, Robert and I went on to forge a friendship that eventually led to him getting me to appear on TV's Tony Brown's Journal.

I wrote hundreds, if not thousands, of posts. Some just a few words, some complete essays. I have hundreds boxed away, not opened in years. I feel I have something to say but have not been discovered by the mainstream media. In fact, the Black media never opened up to me, even though I tried.

I did a demo tape for WLIB radio in NY. I did so well that the Director said, “You are no amateur”. Yet, I was never hired. Perhaps that is the price you pay for challenging the powers that be.

This is a collection of thoughts, letters, essays and poems. I want to leave a record of my work.

May God Bless and Keep You!

Introduction

God gifted me with the ability to speak and write. I have tried to use my talents for the betterment of my people.

Louis Farrakhan once said, “If we could take what we learned in corporate America, we could free our people overnight.” He also went on to say that we would be resented. I lived through this.

Some thought I would become Harlem’s Congressman and a national leader. Yet what my Mother taught me about education and hard work did not sit well with many. My Mother worked three jobs and did sleep-away work. In this work, she came home one day a week. Many laughed at her as they sat on the garbage can all day waiting on a welfare check. Many of my people are stuck in a welfare mentality, waiting on the “white man” and “Gument” to provide for them.

Since I have been ignored by the media and the powers that be, I am putting out the first volume of my book of essays, letters, and poems and thoughts to leave it as a record for the next generation.

How this is received will dictate if there is a volume 2.

I have a lot to say!

Open Letter to President Biden

Maurice G. Faucette

718-324-3720

January 20, 2021

I trust this letter makes it past your screeners to your desk. Congratulations on your election as Our President!

I wrote last June 2020 to Speaker Nancy Pelosi, as well as Representative Claiborne, Meeks, the late John Lewis Congressional Black Chair Karen Bass and several others, and I was ignored.

As a "Private" in the Democratic Party, I wrote to the "Officers" asking why they had endorsed Eliot Engel as the Democratic nominee for the NY 16th Congressional Seat. I know you guys are tasked with the big picture as to what must be done to get more for people nationwide. In order to have a better understanding of the quid pro quo of congressional politics and seniority, I wanted them to tell me, an ordinary Black man, why I should vote for Eliot Engel.

I, like many Black people, have put my trust and faith in the Democratic Party. I feel, as a Black voter, that my vote is being taken for granted. The Black vote, in a record turn out, put you over the top. What are you going to do for the ordinary, everyday Black

Person in America who voted for you against Donald Trump? Naming Cabinet members of color is one thing, but what are the masses going to get for delivering the Presidency to you? We are beyond symbolism and ‘‘tokenism.

I live in the 16th Congressional District in the Northwest part of an area of the Bronx called Wakefield. This Northwest part of Wakefield may as well be called the "Homeless Shelter" capital of NYC. This area has Democratic elected. Officials at every level of government except for President Trump, until today January 20th, I now have Democratic representation at every level. Despite assurances from the local elected officials, including Eliot Engel, that a "Homeless Shelter" would not be opened at 4747 Bronx Blvd, one has opened. How can the City of NY open a shelter without the blessing of the Democratic powers that be?

Additionally, Eliot Engel gave the vacant federal property, the Mueller Army Center on Nereid Avenue, to a non-profit to open up another Homeless Shelter less than 500 feet from an existing shelter. This means there will be three large Homeless Shelters within 4.5 blocks of each other. This area, where People of color worked multiple jobs to purchase 1-3 family homes, is starting to resemble the old Bowery, with males from the shelter loitering, panhandling, and even sleeping on the sidewalk.

Eliot Engel must have had a lot of Congressional power and

influence due to his seniority, as I received tons of "robo calls". Many were from the Westchester part of the district lauding his accomplishments. My mailbox was full of campaign literature. If he had been re-elected, most likely, we would not have heard from him until again until 2022. I have no doubt now that with 100% Democratic representation, from the City Council to the President, more homeless shelters will be opened in Wakefield. By the way, if you see Jamal Bowman, the new Congressman, please ask him to visit the Wakefield part of the district in the Bronx. Wakefield has reached out to him during the campaign and since the election with no response. Perhaps being from Westchester, the Bronx, is not important!

I feel shelters are being dumped here in Wakefield so as not to put them in the white areas in the NYC part of the district. The Carpenter Avenue group has fought this with little political support from the elected officials. Apparently, Commissioner Banks of the Department of Homeless Services. answers to no politician, including the Mayor, and he can put shelters anywhere he pleases.

As it turned out, the race was not even close, and despite all the Washington Democratic support, Engel lost. For the record, what I asked for from the Democrats who controlled my district at every level except the Presidency was ignored, or they implied they could do nothing about it. It seems like they wanted me to think it was Trump's fault like everything wrong in my district was Trump's fault. Now, since you are President with Democratic representation at every level of Government, please grant this loyal Democratic Base of People of color the following:

1. Immediate cancellation of the contract for the shelter at 4747 Bronx Blvd. The immediate closure of the shelter.

2. The Mueller Center is to be returned to the Community and converted into a Youth Center with athletic, educational, cultural, media and theater arts facilities

3. If the Mueller Center must be a Homeless Shelter for Veterans, I want it to be built as a condominium and ownership to be given to the veterans. I believe they will help to build this community with pride of ownership as opposed to pulling down the character and fiber of the neighborhood as the shelter on Bronx Blvd near Nereid is doing.

President Biden, I personally invite you and all Members of the Congressional Black Caucus to visit Wakefield, the "Homeless Shelter" Capital of NYC, to see for you how we are being dumped on.

Additionally, I believe there should be a re-redistricting of Wakefield, part of an all-Bronx district. The interests of the Bronx do not match some of the affluent areas of Westchester.

Yes, I have Democratic representation at all levels of

Government, including you, the President and despite our loyalty, we get Homeless Shelters.

Maurice G. Faucette

Enclosed is a copy of the letter I sent to Nancy Pelosi!

Open Letter

June 18, 2020

Nancy Pelosi

Speaker of the House of Representatives

Members of the Congressional Black Caucus

I trust this letter makes it past your screeners to your desk. As a "Private" in the Democratic Party, I write to the "Officers" asking why you have endorsed Eliot Engel as the Democratic nominee for the NY 16th Congressional Seat. I know you are tasked with the big picture as to what must be done to get more for people nationwide. In order to have a better understanding of the quid pro quo of congressional politics and seniority, I want you to tell me, an ordinary Black man, why I should vote for him.

I, like many Black people, have put my trust and faith in the Democratic Party. I feel, as a Black voter, that my vote has been taken for granted.

I live in the 16th Congressional District in the Northwest part of an area of the Bronx called Wakefield. This Northwest part of Wakefield may as well be called the "Homeless Shelter" capital of NYC. **<u>This area has Democratic elected officials at every level of government except for the President.</u>** Despite assurances from the local elected officials, including Eliot Engel, that a "Homeless Shelter" would not be opened at 4747 Bronx Blvd, one has opened. How can the City of NY open a shelter without the blessing of the Democratic powers that be?

Additionally, Eliot Engel gave the vacant federal property, the Mueller Army Center on Nereid Avenue, to a non-profit to open up another Homeless Shelter less than 500 feet from an existing shelter. This means there will be 3 large Homeless Shelters within 4.5 blocks of each other. This area, where People of color worked multiple jobs to purchase 1-3 family homes, is starting to resemble the old Bowery, with males from the shelter loitering, panhandling, and even sleeping on the sidewalk.

Now, Eliot Engel must have a lot of Congressional power and influence due to his seniority, as I am getting tons of robo calls, many from the Westchester part of the district, lauding his accomplishments. My mailbox is full of campaign literature. If he is re-elected, will we not hear from him again until 2022, while more shelters are opened here?

I feel shelters are being dumped here in Wakefield so as not to put them in the white areas in the NYC part of the district. The Carpenter Avenue group will be meeting this Saturday @ 1:00 to discuss closing the shelter. Please send a representative.

The race is close, and there are enough votes in Wakefield to swing it either way. If you want me to vote for Engel in the June 23rd Democratic primary, this is what I want.

1. Immediate cancellation of the contract for the shelter at 4747 Bronx Blvd. The immediate closure of the shelter.

2. The Mueller Center is to be returned to the Community and converted into a Youth Center with athletic, educational, cultural, media and theater arts facilities

3. If the Mueller Center must be a Homeless Shelter for Veterans, I want it to be built as a condominium and ownership to be given to the veterans. I believe they will help to build this. Community with pride of ownership as opposed to pulling down the character and fiber of the neighborhood as the shelter on Bronx Blvd near Nereid is doing.

Nancy Pelosi, I personally invite all Members of the Congressional Black Caucus to visit Wakefield, the "Homeless Shelter" Capital of NYC, to see for you how we are being dumped on.

Additionally, I believe there should be a re-redistricting of Wakefield, part of an all-Bronx district. The interests of the Bronx do not match some of the affluent areas of Westchester.

Yes, I have Democratic representation at all levels of Government except for the President, and despite my loyalty, we get Homeless Shelters.

Maurice G. Faucette

718-324-3720

#JamalBowman

#EliotEngel

#NancyPelosi

#Congressional Black Caucus

The Legal Case for Reparations

Maurice G. Faucette

Ask anyone how a human owns a building, land or anything of value, and you will get a wide range of answers. Many will talk of the acquisition method or means, such as cash, mortgages, contracts and other means. Yet the technical, spiritual answer is that humans cannot own anything. They can only use what God has created while on this earth. Ashes to ashes, dust to dust, whatever comes from the earth must return.

The fact of the matter is that humans own property because a government has issued, endorsed and enforced through blood, sweat and tears a document, a deed, or a stock certificate that. says that a human owns that property. As long as that Government stays in power and enforces such, then that human owns that property. When there is a new government, as evidenced when the Nazis took control of Germany and Castro took control of Cuba, the documents were not enforced and humans lost their property with virtually no recourse.

Man evolved to paper ownership, as evidenced in John Locke's Essay on Government. He stated that Man would evolve from being uncivilized to being civilized, then eventually back to being uncivilized. He said civilization would not work. In an uncivilized society, there were no deeds. A human "owned" wherever a stake could be put in the ground, and he could claim through sheer blunt force. Much blood was shed to protect this stake, and man eventually evolved into civilization, and now a deed enforceable by the government said this human owned it.

The system of deeds was put in place in the United States of America at a time when the descendants of captured Africans who had been kidnapped and brought to America to work against their will, without compensation were not considered Men and Women. They were not allowed to participate in this system of government. These paper proofs of ownership backed by the blood, sweat and tears of the descendants of these Africans, who have fought American Wars, are allowed to be passed down from generation to generation without any remuneration or compensation to the descendants of those kidnapped and forced under threat of death to work for free.

Many today holding wealth in America do so, holding the proceeds of the worst crime in American History! The crime of kidnapping and holding African humans against their will. A crime for which no compensation has been paid!

Under American Law, proceeds derived from an illegal criminal enterprise can be seized or forfeited! As a result, based on the crimes of their ancestors and the fact that these deeds have been passed from generation to generation with no compensation, the deeds need to be invalidated and the proceeds distributed to the descendants of the African humans who were kidnapped, and forced to work under the threat of death for free.

Yet, I am a realist, and the best lawyers from the best firms will be stifled in the courts and the media, with virtually no support from the powers that be, the media or the government, as power and control of wealth is ruthless and absolute. Those with the wealth as inherited by the sins of their forefathers will do everything possible to dispute and stop this. Many are Machiavellian, and if Machiavelli could give credence to cutting a baby like Jesus' throat in the crib just because he posed a future threat to power. You can deduce what will be done to protect this wealth.

I could turn to the government to enforce this, but I have little hope. Many of the elected officials are little more than coins in the pocket of the powers that be, as Vito Corleone held, as was depicted by Barziniin the movie "The GodFather". Many times, we know the King, but we do not know the Kingmaker. The Kingmakers control the wealth, and the politicians kiss the ring of the Kingmaker. I can see it now going up to the Supreme Court with Clarence Thomas casting the deciding vote. So I offer America a compromise, a grant to Black America equal to 2-3 Xs the latest stimulus package... That is the easy part. The tough part will be how to distribute. Please do not put it in the hands of the Black Politicians, Ministers and "Bougie Black Leaders" because I am not sure it will reach the masses. Please do not laugh, but did not Adam Clayton Powell Jr, bring tons of money into Harlem. Money that was stolen and funneled to children who did not live in Harlem.

I propose a committee of Educators to come up with a distribution formula based on genealogy to the Great Grand Parent level. One of the complaints of Black People who have been here for generations, like my Family, is that many people of color come here and do not want to be identified as Black until it benefits them. I am pretty sure many will want a cut. No offense, but those who can trace their ancestry through generations of abuse here in America deserve more than those who just got here or their ancestors since the battles were fought for civil rights in places like Alabama, where my Mother was born and raised.

Please do not take offense and you can take it as satire or fact, but reparations can be the nastiest drag-down fight.

Dark Skinned niggas are going to want more than lite-sinned niggas, American born, more than the. West Indians, the Southerners more than the Northerners, the Kappas more than the Ques, Democrats more than the Republicans, and you know the Ministers want a bigger cut because the Buffer Class got to get theirs.

On a simple note, maybe give the Black Colleges an endowment to give free education to Children of Color or Allow People of Color an interest-free or reduced rate of interest mortgage with no credit check to buy a home.

0% 15-year mortgages for all descendants proving the # of their Great-grandparents born in the United States of America. You could divide into 8 groups, based on the # proven to have been born here. on a sliding scale.

Laugh, dismiss, but based on the amount of money, come up with something better!

May Peace be unto you!

Defund The Police or Not?

The Will of The People

President Joseph Biden

Vice President Kamala Harris

US Senate

US House of Representatives

Police or No Police, Defunding or Increased Funding, It is what the American People want. To all the Elected Officials, You represent the People. You do our bidding. You answer to Us.

That is the fundamental thing wrong with America today. The Elected Officials have become elitists; They think They know what is best for us. They must listen to what the people want. Do they answer to the People, or do they answer to lobbyists, PACs, campaign contributors and special interests?

The Police were not intended to be the tool of the Elitist so as to protect the Elitist or do the bidding of the Elitist so as to keep The Elitist in Power. John Locke's Essay on government details man's evolution from being uncivilized to being civilized. John Locke said, "Civilization would not work, and man would evolve back to being uncivilized. **Are we seeing this evolution in action?** Is the evolution starting with Donald Trump a President saying,

"There will be no defunding" just because he says so? That is the fundamental reason why America is where it is today. An elected official, the President of the United States, who will not listen to or respect the will of the American people, A President intent on dividing this country rather than uniting. A President who thinks He knows what is best for America based on his own selfish interests.

To both Democrats and Republicans, you have become separated from the masses. With a few exceptions, many spend most all their time in Washington, not with their constituents. Some question as to whether some congresspersons and senators even live in the district they represent. Granted, there is someplace in their district with their name on a lease or deed so as to claim residency so as to be eligible to run.

An elected official, former Congressman Eliot Engel, was up for re-election who reportedly had not visited His District for 3 months during the pandemic. At an event back in his home area, on an open "mic," Elliot Engel is heard saying, He would not be here if He was not running for reelection. Please be reminded, all elected officials, that you are running for election, and the seat does not belong to you. Many of the elected officials think it belongs to them.

Joe Biden, while I will give my vote to the Democratic candidate for President, in my opinion, the incumbent (Trump at the time this was written) is not an option. I am not sure you are the one to make government work for this one Black Man. Yet I understand why Black Americans must vote together as a block.

To win by default is one thing; to win by earning it is another. As a Black Man, I feel the Democratic Party has taken my people for granted. The Democratic Party gives the Black Community virtually no patronage for our vote. That is a fundamental rule of politics, along with protocol. The patronage We do get is usually social programs. **The ills of the community the Social Funding is supposed to resolve are not resolved and the problems seem to increase. I ask myself, as a Black Man, was the intent ever to solve the problems? Is it to provide patronage under the disguise of helping?**

Look at the "Homeless" problem in New York City. There is no intent, will, program or strategy to solve it. The spending is making millionaires of those throwing up buildings everywhere to house the homeless. Is it wise to spend thousands per month to house the homeless in hotels? Is the intent to house the homeless or to provide patronage? The intent is definitely not to solve the homeless crisis because it is getting worse. Developers are building shelters every without regard to the wants or needs of the community. They get top dollar from DHS, NYC's Department of Homeless Services.

DHS is giving contract after contract, stacking People in old converted warehouses and feeding them meals that cost virtually nothing.

Yes, the Democrats have taken my vote and, in my opinion, most of Black America for granted. History should teach The Democrats that their arrogance, overconfidence and cavalier attitude towards Black America cost Hillary the 2016 election. The Democrats lost three States by 76 00 votes. Hillary lost Michigan by 10,000 votes alone. **Research shows there were 2,000,000 fewer Black voters in 2016, than showed out for Barrack.** Black people turning out to vote in 2016, in Detroit alone could have delivered Michigan to Hillary. She needed Black voter turnout at the levels that put Barrack in office. Black voter turnout at 2016 levels in Philadelphia, Pittsburgh, Allentown, and Harrisburg, would have delivered Pennsylvania to Hillary.

In any contest, whether it is football, basketball or politics, when you go into the 4th quarter and there is an insurmountable margin, like 50 points, it is virtually over. In a game where the lead is within reach, like 7-14 points, how you play the game in the 4th quarter will dictate winning or losing. Ask the 49ers and Falcons, who lost Super Bowls. Now, let us look at Hillary. In spite of all the Russian stuff, Benghazi, her elitist attitude that did little to energize the Democratic base, specifically Black voters, going down the stretch, Hillary had a chance to win., A heretofore **own American polls showed a 7- 14 point lead.** ***The Republicans' foreign pollster, let me repeat foreign pollster from another country said the race was a dead heat.*** So you have two camps looking at two different scoreboards. Overconfident, the Democrats did nothing to energize the base. Elections are won in the 4th quarter based on turnout, not on flipping voters, not on getting the undecided votes, but on turnout. The Democrats invested very little down the stretch resources because The Democrats were overconfident, arrogant and, rather than going into the Black inner cities and putting resources on the street, the **overconfident Democrats did little to energize the Black vote to go to the poll and the Democrats lost.**

You would think that the Democrats have learned to respect the Black Voter more, but have they? We want more than social programs. **Black America is not all poor and broke, down on our knees begging**. That may be what some so-called Black/ Hispanic and White elected officials are telling You. We are a Proud People. We built this Nation. We held our Families together against all odds. Most Black Americans are people who get up and go to work, but the Democrats keep catering to the poor so as to provide patronage to their campaign donors and to answer to the lobbyists because, in spite of all the dollars, the problems exist and, in fact, are getting worse.

I will close this essay by telling you, Joe Biden, what I am just an everyday Black Man who, because I am such you, may not even read this article. See, I am not an elected official, I am not a minister, I am not a celebrity, nor do I have a big fat check to give you. Most likely, one of your screeners has intercepted this, and they sent me a form letter as a response. If you have read this far, let me tell you how disappointed I am in the Democratic Party.

My home is in the Wakefield section of the North Bronx; Wakefield is becoming the Homeless Capital of NYC. Shelters are being built all over. The neighborhood is starting to resemble "The Bowery" back in the day. I **am represented by Democrats at every level of "Gument" except for the President.** Wakefield is a Community of People of Color. I believe the Shelters are being put in Wakefield because **they will never put them in the white parts of the district., like Riverdale.**

This entire Democratic representation from the City Council to the Congressman, to 2 US Senators and the Governor gave the "Dough" Fund, excuse me, The Doe Fund, the old Mueller Military Center, to build another shelter less than 500 feet from another shelter. Do you really think this is about the Homeless?

This is about political patronage and the arrogant policies of the NY Democratic Party, which does not care about Black People like me. Why are shelters being dumped where People of color live?

In fact, another shelter just opened at 4747 Bronx Blvd. in Wakefield. The Democratic elected officials from the City Council Member have said they were told the building would not be opened as a Homeless Shelter. Am I to believe that DHS, which answers to a Democratic Mayor, did this on its own? Does the Mayor and all the local elected officials who cover the area, from the City Council Member up to the Congressman, have no control over DHS?

This Black Man believes my people have been made the sacrificial lamb of the American economy. Students of Economics know You cannot have 0% unemployment. Inflation would be off the chart. Some people have to not work to make this Economic. System of Keynesian economics work. Hedge Funds skyrocket and leveraged real estate investments make millionaires overnight.

The proliferation of Shelters in Wakefield, an area covered by Democratic at every level of Government except for the Presidency, is a testimony to the total disrespect and treatment by the Democratic Party towards this one Black Man.

No, I did not get an invitation to the Fund Raiser at Ciprianni hosted by the Doe Fund for The Elite "Do Gooders", raising money to flood Wakefield with more shelters. **It is not good to go to a**

public hearing with the "Dough" Fund, I mean Doe Fund and while you,(I) have filed to speak, to see the public Hearing about to close without letting me speak. The deal was already in the bag. **HPD, DHS sat and laughed and grinned with the "Dough" Fund, especially their arrogant and, in my opinion, racist Director of Development,** who damn near laughed in my face after I spoke. They let me speak, but nobody listened.

See, if a residence for Homeless Veterans is to be built, why not Condominiums? Why not give them a "piece of the Rock"? They served this country; They have their blood, sweat, and tears. They saw friends pay the ultimate sacrifice.

Yet my proposal was laughed at. The "Dough" Fund, excuse me, Doe Fund, would not have it's revenue stream not under their control. See**, this was and is not about the Homeless but about money and political patronage.** Remember, this Black Man was represented at every level of government, with the exception of the President, by Democrats. I feel they do not care how I feel. Now, I have 100% representation at every level, and I have little hope things will change.

Will the Democrats ever write and pass legislation that there be no funding in any form for Homeless, low-income, or Subsidized Housing unless there are apprenticeship programs employing young people of color, who need work and live in the community? To have an outside workforce come into the inner city to build low and middle-income housing without rebuilding the economy is both counterproductive and is more about political patronage than helping the People.

We need the economy of the Black/Latino inner City rebuilt, and we will build our own homes. We will re/circulate the money to make jobs. Maybe if some of the Buildings in the inner city were given to so-called **Youth Gangs** to fix up rather than to the same old **Reverend Chicken Bones** who slap their names on them, get all kinds of subsidies that have to go through them, we could solve the problems in our communities. If the Democratic Party, along with the US Government, would "get off our necks" and let us breathe, we could find common ground and realistic solutions to solve our problems.

We must make sure the intent of all Federal Funding is to Build and Liberate People of color and not political patronage to ensure re-election.

I close by saying I voted against Trump by voting for Biden/Harris as part of the **"Black Voting Bloc."** I know you will never visit Wakefield in the North Bronx. I have no million-dollar campaign contribution. I voted for you because Trump is not an option for this Black Man.

The President (Trump) claims He did so much for Black

America. **Economic Boom Bust Cycles** were here on the face of the Earth before the Trump Organization was discriminating against Black people in housing in Brooklyn.

Politicians take credit for the natural boom-bust cycles when things are good and blame the bad on their opponents. This cycle for prosperity was put in place by the President's who's Portrait Trump will not hang, a Man who ran when others did not, a Man who took over America's leadership in the midst of one of the worst economic bust cycles due to both natural and man-made reasons. Trump is simply riding on the wave that the President, whose portrait he will not hang, started.

President Joseph Biden, Vice President Kamala Harris, US Senate, US House of Representatives,

I invite You to Wakefield, a Community of Color, a Community of 1, 2, and 3 Family Homes, where People with Southern and Caribbean Roots live, where People who have built Homes with pennies saved by working 2 and 3 jobs like My Mother who wrote to Presidents, sweat equity", down payments from Sou Sou's to live in a nice neighborhood.

Where We have believed in a Democratic Party that has not truly lived up to the rhetoric, I ask that you and the Democratic Party be all that You can be!

May God Bless and Keep You on this journey.

Maurice G. Faucette

Open letter to the Hess family

I would appreciate it if you could contact the ownership of Speedway and tell them that it would be wise to keep your stations up to the standards that the Hess family had under your ownership. The stations under your leadership had a clean bathroom policy. The stations were clean, but more importantly, the Hess Family had a care for the community.

I live across the street from one of your stations in the Bronx, and a couple of times, under the Hess family leadership, I had issues with the conditions at the station! I called the executive offices, and I asked for the Executive Assistant to Mr. Hess. While I did not get a chance to speak to Mr. Hess, The executive assistant, who was very nice, kind, and professional, took down my information.

Within a couple of hours, I got a response. For example, one was about a cargo container sitting at the Hess station Nereid the Bronx, and there was some type of noise coming from it. I could hear the noise in the middle of the night. I made a noise complaint to the city of New York. They came out and did nothing.

When I called the Hess offices and made a complaint, there was somebody out at the station within two hours. Whatever was making that noise was disconnected. Now let me take you to the speedway on the way there.

The former Hess station on Nereid is now a Speedway. The Speedway is right around the corner from a homeless shelter on Bronx Boulevard. The guys from the homeless shelter hang out at the speedway. They hang out at the station. They ask people if they can buy pump gas. They panhandle at the station and on the corner.

The station station is not kept as clean as it used to be under the Hess family's leadership the biggest problem is on the Carpenter Avenue side, where people have used it as a garbage dump. People are literally dumping “contractors” waste and garbage all over the sidewalk.

Graffiti, which the station personnel used to clean religiously, is now being left. It is an eyesore. I don't know if the manager was getting tired of cleaning it up. I don't know if the manager getting tired of the garbage because the garbage sits for days.

The Hess family no longer has an interest in this property. You are a great corporate citizen. I ask that you contact Speedways leadership and implore upon them to clean up this station.

You may say contact them directly. I have made several contacts with no response! Speedway is a multi-million billion-dollar corporation, and they have the financial and political resources to stop this. They seem to be totally unconcerned. I have made complaints, and I get no response. The problems get worse. The Hess family, maybe if you impress upon them the meaning of being a good corporate citizen and leading by example, they will do something. I wonder that since the North Bronx area of Wakefield is no longer a predominantly white neighborhood, but one of people of color, that maybe Speedway thinks it does not have to do anything!

The North Bronx Bronx is beginning to become a slum due to the negligence of corporations like Speedway.

This negligence and lack of care well as the lack of response by the political leadership in New York only, only makes the situation worse.

I ask the Hess Family to contact Speedway and ask them to clean up the situation! Ask them to ask them to be a great corporate citizen like Hess is!

May Peace be with the Hess Family!

I elevated this up the ladder to the parent corp. of 7/11 and 7i Corp in Japan. Action has been taken to resolve most of the issues. I thank those who took action.

Letter to Major League Baseball

Rob Manfred MLB Commissioner.

MLB Owners

Major league baseball right now has a problem with decreasing offensive production. The number of strikeouts and low-scoring games is increasing.

Unlike the NBA and NFL, which have made numerous rule changes over the years so as to maintain a competitive balance and interest of fans, the best baseball can come up with is checking the pitchers for foreign substances or devices to make marks on the ball.

MLB has also eliminated the need to throw 4 pitches to make for 4-0 intentional walks. You can just send the batter to 1st base.

Making a mark or indentation on the ball makes it do aerodynamically different things. The ball will twist and turn more than an unaltered baseball. This additional motion makes a baseball more difficult to follow with the eye and more difficult to hit. It makes hand-eye coordination, which is a fundamental part of hitting, much more difficult.

Athletes are involved with and get better with new technology, training methods and nutrition.

In baseball, pitching is evolving faster than hitting. A picture only needs a catcher or catching/accuracy device to practice.

This, along with focused exercising, have made pitchers throw harder and more accurate. This, as a result, has caused the number of strikeouts to increase. Baseball is concerned. It advertises offense, particularly **Home Runs.** The offensive numbers have dropped over the years. Many think that Baseball looked the other way when steroids increased human performance, resulting in more home runs and more fans in the seats and watching on TV.

Then, there is a question as to of the limits of the human body. How fast can a human throw, and how much time does a human need to react. The pitchers are evolving faster towards their human limits but have a ways to go. Estimates are that the top speeds for a human arm are 108-110 mph. Many are throwing over 100 mph in MLB. It is no longer a rarity.

How much more can the human body improve reaction time for a ball traveling over 100 miles per hour over a distance of 60'6"? It may already be there, giving pitchers the advantage.

Many years ago, it was a comedy article in the media when the highest average in the American League was. .299. It alluded to averages being so low that a batter got his 1st hit of the season and won the batting crown.

There are only a couple of rule changes. in my opinion, to improve the art of hitting, that MLB Baseball should make. That will probably solve the problem for the next 10 to 12 years because things will progress, and then there will be some other type of rule changes.

I don't agree with moving the mound back. Basketball, for example, with it's own issues of marketability have talked about moving the basket to 12 feet, but it has not. They have made adjustments on the time to shoot both on the initial possession and on the offensive rebounds. Years ago, it did away with hand checking so as to maintain some type of competitive balance.

The first thing baseball is to take a look at is that most of the fans watch the game on TV. I don't know what the numbers are. They don't pay me to calculate. Even when many people go to the game, they watch a broadcast while there.

So many times, batters have strikes called against when the ball does not touch the strike zone. The video replay shows the fans that the umpire missed it. Many of the misses are not by an inch or two but several inches. Pitchers have mastered nipping corners and trying to get batters to swing at pitchers out of the strike zone. Yet when pitching is dominating hitting, there needs to be a change to balance this out.

Make the pitchers put the ball in the hitting zone by eliminating "nipping" the corners. The umpires will only call strikes if the ball is 100% over the plate. This will incent pitchers to throw more pitches in the hitting zone. I also believe it will incent pitchers to throw more fastballs. I think this will bring a better balance for the foreseeable future between pitchers and hitters.

Next rule modification. MLB wanted to speed up the game by doing away with the need to throw pitches to give a batter the intentional walk. It saves a minute or two. Yet, for over a century, it has been an advantage for the defense to avoid a top hitter or hitter favorable situation.

Of the major sports, baseball is the only game where you cannot put the offense consistently in the hands of your best scorer or play maker. In Baseball, your best hitter has to wait for 8 other players to bat. You can have Micheal Jordan take 30 shots, Jim Brown to carry the ball 30 times, but in baseball, Mickey Mantle only gets 4 at bats most games. Then you come to the game, and Mickey Mantle gets walked.

How do you modify the intentional walk or all walks? Staying as close to the game for the purists, make it so if you walk a batter 4-0, the runners on base advance also.

Or you can award the batter 2 bases. If the batter is walked 4-0. So Mantle comes up with runners on 2nd and 3rd, there is no longer an empty base as we know it. The runners will score if you walk Mantle 4-0. Four balls and no strikes. This gives Micky Mantle at least one pitch to hit. To really eliminate the defensive advantage of the intentional walk and to force pitchers to throw the ball over the plate, why not make all walks 2 bases. Before you say no, does the new extra-inning rule to place a runner on 2nd base tell you anything?

If you make all walks 2 bases, this will force pitchers to throw the ball over the plate. This will make base runners more aggressive. More aggressive base runners cause pitchers to be not as focused. Pitchers will throw more pitches in the hitting zone. I believe pitchers will throw more fastballs. MLB will not even read this less more make changes.

So people all over America will drive to see their favorite player hit and he gets walked because he is an offensive threat. You go figure!

The same Old MLK Jr. Speeches

Maurice G. Faucette

I am not a politician, minister, rapper, or famous person, but if our youth have to hear the same old MLK loves somebody rhetoric again, less and less of them will listen. I want to deliver my General King and the Battle of Montgomery somewhere. I may be critical, but the sermon I heard Sunday about put me to sleep. I felt he was preaching to the nonbelievers, not the people in church. Then too there were mostly women. Few young black males were in attendance. Sometime in 2017, I am going to do my Message to The Black Man Speech or maybe take the time to speak out.

31 years ago, one of the most prominent Black Ministers in America said he would be my King Maker. Two Women close to me told me he would do nothing because I would outshine him. Black Preachers are protective of their turf. Someone has been really pushing me lately, like my brother disclosed to me 40 years ago. So if someone is having something...

Introduction to General King and the Battle of Montgomery

Maurice G. Faucette

I am tired of people criticizing Martin Luther King Jr. and the use of non-violence without knowing jack shit as to why he did it! Read his book "Desegregation At Last". The story of the Montgomery Bus Boycott! He was 26 years old! He was asked to lead because he was new to Montgomery! He was up against a nasty, vicious enemy, and any attempt at violence would have led to disastrous consequences for our people!

General King defeated a far superior enemy, an enemy with superior manpower, armament, and courts, with minimal casualties. Gandhi led a movement in which the Indians outnumbered the British 7-1!

General King and the Battle of Montgomery is a paper I wrote after I was the guest speaker at a church 20 years ago! I will post on his birthday! I would love to deliver it, but the churches only want the usual Dr. King said to love somebody BS!

"For non-violence to be effective, you must be violent! Nonviolence is not to protect the cowards"!

In celebration of the birthday I submit for your review my paper: **"General King and The Battle of Montgomery".** It is attached for your downloading. I wrote this because non-violence is a very misunderstood concept. The question is, can non-violence beat a violent enemy? I wrote this because of the book, **"Stride Toward Freedom"**: The Montgomery Bus Boycott Story by Martin Luther King, Jr.

I was the keynote speaker at a church in New Jersey for Martin Luther King Day back in the 1990's. The essay was a result of that speech from which I have expanded into this article.

General King and The Battle of Montgomery

Maurice G. Faucette

We are at a time of year where Dr. Martin Luther King Jr.'s life is discussed. Some are very critical of non-violence, and some preach non-violence in their rhetoric while their actions say otherwise.

The ultimate Samurai warrior is taught that he will do everything possible to defeat his enemy without pulling his sword from his sheath. If he has no choice other than to resort to violence, it must be quick, decisive, and absolute.

Dr. King's tactics and strategies are like warfare and football, and the Monday morning quarterbacks who second guess decisions after the fact in the comfort of their living room. When you stand shoulder to shoulder with me, facing the enemy at the moment of truth, you are qualified to ask me "why I did what I did".

You be the general chosen to fight the battle of Montgomery. You decide a battle plan, against a nasty, vicious enemy. An enemy that has control over the police, the courts, and the media. An enemy that outnumbers you 100 to 1.

Prepare yourself; read books about war, like "The Art of War", "The Book of Five Rings". Go to West Point or Annapolis and interview all the top Generals & Admirals. "You do not engage a superior enemy in a battle of force". The Art of War states, "If you know yourself, but not your enemy, for every victory there will be a defeat. If you know yourself, and your enemy, you will not be fearful in a thousand battles."

Understand what happened in Vietnam. Understand **guerrilla warfare**. Understand the macho mentality of frontal assaults. Understand the pullback tactics used by the Russians in WWII to defeat the Germans. Understand that over two hundred years earlier, Napoleon got trapped by the winter under similar circumstances, as the German Army. Understand Custer's personal ambition and the trap laid for him at Little Big Horn. Understand the decision of President Truman to drop 2 atomic bombs because he knew the enemy. **An enemy where their own warrior Bushido code demanded that the Japanese Generals not surrender even after the second bomb was dropped.** Understand why Field Marshall Rommel said the Allies had to be stopped at the beach. Understand why the Vietcong lost the military part of the Tet Offensive but won the media battle as public pressure mounted for the USA to pull out. Understand why the Black Massachusetts soldiers pictured in the movie "Glory" lost the battle but won the war, as the fort was never taken.

Then once again, after all your studying, you be General King, 26 years of age, put in command because you are new to the area. You be Dr. King, up against an enemy that outnumbers you, an enemy with superior armor, an enemy with the police force, the judges, and the courts all stacked against you. Dr. King knew himself and he knew the enemy. I ask people what they know about Dr. King other than what the media has displayed. What do they know about Dr. King? What have they read and studied on their own? Dr. King was educated. He understood the power of the media. He understood common decency. He was educated to realize the media is controlled by those who may or may not have your interests at heart. He knew that the powers that be control the masses through labels.

That poor whites and poor blacks were both victimized by the same oppressor. As long as they were at odds with each other, the oppressor would never be challenged. Jesus knew this and had to be stopped by the powers that be, so did Gandhi, who was stopped and soon Malcolm X would meet the same fate. **In fact, the oppressor is so masterful he can get those the architect is trying to help to destroy the architect, the dreamer, out of their own ignorance and shallow jealousy.** History repeats itself time after time.

General King was the architect of one of the greatest victories in the 20th century. Despite being outnumbered and outgunned, he brought a superior enemy to their knees with a minimum number of casualties. He brought a superior enemy to their knees who had infiltrated his officer ranks and had them trying to disrupt and sell him and the movement out.

His major strategy to defeat this superior enemy was nonviolence. I recommend to all who want to better understand Dr. King's decision to read Stride Toward Freedom: The Montgomery Story by Martin Luther King, Jr.

Two of the best educated, best-read men of the 20th century were Malcolm X and Dr. Martin Luther King Jr. Monday morning history quarterbacks who criticize and second guess them have never read 1/100 of the material that Malcolm X and Dr. Martin Luther King Jr. read. In his book **"Stride Towards Freedom"** the story of the Montgomery Bus Boycott, Dr. King devotes an entire chapter to his philosophical journey. Dr. King did not come up with this philosophy overnight. He read books by philosopher after philosopher.

King spoke of the "theory of the soulful force", the power of the human spirit. "The human will is more power full than any physical force on Earth".

Dr. King studied Gandhi and his principles of non-violence. "To truly be non-violent, you must be violent". The non-violent concept is not to protect the coward. "If you have to choose between cowardice and violence, choose violence." These are the words of Gandhi. The power of looking an enemy in the eye, that you have the will, desire, the propensity to kill, and having enough strength, love, and compassion not to, makes non-violence effective. Yes, it is painful, yes, it is not easy. As Jesus said, "Father, let this cup pass, not by my will but by yours."

This type of discipline is what makes elite military units effective. The ultimate Samurai warrior is taught to do everything possible to defeat his enemy without pulling his sword from his sheath.

Dr. King understood that everything translates into economics as the first law of man's hierarchy of needs, as evidenced by Maslow, is food, clothing and shelter. The economic pressure made the powers to be listen. Green commands attention. The masses think it is about white and black. Money is not the root of all evil. Money is a medium of exchange. The pursuit of money without regards to God and common decency is the root of evil. Dr. King spoke out about the Vietnam War because it was the profit motivation funneled through lobbyists that fueled the war. It was not a doctrine of liberation. **If it was truly a doctrine of liberation, then the war would have been quick, decisive, and absolute, like a Samurai warrior. Wars motivated by profit funneled by lobbyists drag on.**

The economics drew the battle lines, as the enemy had to fight. The violence against King's disciplined warriors (many, who were the toughest, , w under normal circumstances would have made them violent, Through Jesus's love, they had the power of restraint. Being beaten by the police on camera, launched a media barrage. The pictures went around the world. Until now, the truth, as sent through newspaper and radio reports, allowed America to ignore it. Yet a picture is worth a thousand words, and a film is worth a million pictures. **This publicity pushed the hand of the powers to be as the world watched as the policeman of the world, America, the righteous one, had its dirty laundry displayed around the world.**

This caused money to be pumped in as donations came in to support the boycott. Media coverage intensified. **David was up against Goliath, and Goliath was bigger, tougher, uglier, and more vicious than the world had ever written about.**

The tide of the battle turned. General King's forces held fast. The enemy, notwithstanding the economic burden, started seeing the resources evening out. Th racists were not able to hide behind sheets or the cover of darkness. **The racists taking economic and moral casualties in large numbers, finally succumbed.**

Dr. King, aka General King, was up against a nasty, vicious enemy. He was outnumbered, outgunned, out-manned. With minimum of casualties, Dr. King Jr defeated an enemy who appeared to have everything in their favor.

Dr. King won the Battle of Montgomery. Yet, there were more battles to come. In warfare there is an evolution of tactics and strategies. There are those who felt that he may have stayed with the same tactics and strategies too long. There are those who say he was starting to change and evolve. This evolution and where it may have led is what, in my opinion, got him killed.

May God bless Dr. King as he sits with God Next to Jesus, Moses, Gandhi, and Malcolm.

From Harlem to the Major Leagues?

A Tribute to Jackie Robinson

Maurice G. Faucette

On a cool May morning in 2006, a New York Mets' scout went to a rundown baseball field in Harlem. The stands were splintered; Prostitutes and drug addicts hung around the field. He was there to see a player, a rarity in this day and age, a black inner-city Major League Baseball prospect. The prospect is a 6'3" switch-hitting catcher who played basketball his senior year in high school. not baseball. Recruited by some Division 1 basketball schools, his passion is baseball.

The scout watched, and in the 1st inning, the runner on 1st base took off to steal second. The catcher released the ball. The scout checked his watch and turned to the head of the South Harlem Reds, Maurice Faucets, and said, "Coach, that was a 1.9". 1.9 seconds from the time the throw touched the catcher's glove. This is known as the "Pop Time". He got it out and threw it until it reached the second baseman's glove in 1.9 seconds.. The NY Mets scout talked to his Director of Scouting on the phone. In the second game, the scout told Coach Faucette, "Coach, we get calls on a lot of players, and many times in the first inning, I'm gone. Do you notice I am still here?"

Despite not playing high school baseball, his senior year, Troy Andrews was invited to the NY Mets pre-draft workout at Shea Stadium. He ran the second fastest time in the 60-yard dash and had the best time in the catcher's throw.

But this is about more than Troy Andrews; it is about a group of black men and women in Harlem who believed that with tough love and discipline they could produce in Harlem, baseball players who could play at the high school and college level. They believed that at least one could make it to the major leagues. With all the stories on TV about blacks not playing baseball, the South Harlem Reds, without the support of local politicians or community leaders, set out on a mission to make this happen.

It was in the fall of 1999, the South Harlem Reds 10u pee wee team had played a total of 8 games all summer. Coach Faucette told them he was going to start a fall league. He told them he was going to put them through the meat grinder by putting them up against the best 12u teams in NYC. 10-year-olds against 12-year-olds. He told them that two years later, he expected them to win a national championship in one of the tournaments. He sold them a dream.

The South Harlem Reds got pounded both on the practice field and in games. The losses piled up. 25-0, 24-2, 31-1. Coach Faucette and his staff were relentless. Some players quit, and Coach

Faucette told parents if their baby couldn't handle it, that this was not the place for their child. The South Harlem Reds lost 10 straight. Then, on a warm October day in 1999, the Riverdale Cubs came to Harlem.

A mostly white traveling team with a record of 72-9, no one gave the South Harlem Reds a chance. The white team brought a big crowd out that day in Harlem. In spite of all the losses and all the pounding they had experienced, **the South Harlem Reds that day came to play.** It was the South Harlem Reds against the powerful Riverdale Cubs, and going into the bottom of the 7th, to the amazement of the masses, the South Harlem Reds were leading the Cubs 4-3. With 2 outs. Yet a base-loaded single gave the victory to the Cubs 5-4.

While the players were broken hearted, they found out what "Coach Mo" had been teaching. Through dedication and hard work, they could succeed, not only in baseball but in life. The coach of the Riverdale Cubs, Mark Sherman, a Broadway musician, convinced Coach Faucette to put the South Harlem Reds in several leagues.

In 2000, Coach Faucette decided that the South Harlem Reds would play a 100-game schedule. He also told the kids that if you want to play baseball in New York, you have to play with the Dominicans. And play with the Dominicans they did.

One day, Pat Andrews showed up on the field with her son

Troy. Troy had played against the South Harlem Reds with the Stallions, a Puerto Rican team from East Harlem. He was one of two black players on the Stallions. Anyone who saw Troy at the age of 12 saw his enthusiasm and tenacity. The South Harlem Reds, in honor of Jackie Robinson, gave Troy #42.

The 2000 season was a great one for the South Harlem Reds. Initially, after getting pounded by the Dominican teams in leagues where the umpires spoke no English, the South Harlem Reds got better. Then Coach Faucette had another dream, to win a national tournament.

Coach Faucette contacted Cooperstown Baseball World, which had a fee of $425.00 per player. He asked Debra Sirianni, the Assistant to Eddie Einhorn, the owner for a payment plan. Coach Faucette wanted the kids to sell raffles and wash cars to raise money to pay in installments. He sent several articles to Debra Sirianni on the South Harlem self-help program. What is not mentioned here is that the field the Reds used was a garbage dump, which the Reds made into a baseball field. It was such an accomplishment that Jim Dwyer of the New York Daily News, in his column honoring Jackie Robinson in 1997, said it was done without corporate sponsorship. Jim wrote about Wanda Watson, who picked garbage off the field, who now, years later, is a graduate of Stanford University, with a PHD from Columbia University.

The articles caught the attention of Eddie Einhorn, the founder of Cooperstown Baseball World and one of the owners of the Chicago White Sox. He invited the South Harlem Reds as his guest to play in a tournament. An offer which Coach Faucette initial reaction was to turn down. Coach Faucette was not looking for charity. He eventually accepted, and the Reds went. While they did not win the tournament, they played well, and they were the toast of the town. Everyone fell in love with #42 Troy Andrews.

Then it was back to Harlem and the OLS championship against the 1st place OLS Mets, and their 6'1" intimidating pitcher. A pitcher the South Harlem Reds, gave the name of the "The Big Unit" A pitcher who came to Harlem and struck out 17 batters in a 6-inning game. The pitcher's name is Dillen Betance. That's right, the same Dillen Betance who signed for $1,000,000 with the NY Yankees.

Yet that year, Troy Andrews, 5'5" out, pitched and beat Betances in game 1, 4-1. Troy hit a grand slam in game 2, bringing the South Harlem Reds to within 1. The South Harlem Reds lost game 2, 7-6.. Then it was game three for the title. Troy started, and Dillen did not start, but with the title on the line, Dillen was bought in, and he was hit hard, and the South Harlem Reds were Champions.

At a time when major league teams are not really looking in

the inner city, at a time when the number of black baseball players is decreasing, the South Harlem Reds battle for survival. The city. gave their field to a developer, and it is virtually impossible to get permits as all the politically connected little leagues get them. Some even get private parks, which sit idle most days. Millions of dollars, which some think are going to help the needier kids go to many who have a lot. This is evidenced by players from West Side Little League practicing on a field in Harlem that the Reds are not use. Many of these players from the upper west side travel to the practice with **their nannies carrying their bags.**

Yet, if anyone wants to do a story on Jackie Robinson and why inner-city black kids are playing or not playing baseball, then they need to come talk to those of us who have been in the trenches.

Out of the 20 players who went to Cooperstown in 2000, 15 were black, and 5 were Hispanic. Three of the black players are still playing baseball at a serious level, and oh yeah, Troy is a freshman at Elizabeth City State University in North Carolina. The NY Mets team put him in touch with several high-powered jucos (Junior Colleges). Troy said he wanted to enjoy the college experience. As of Sunday, April 8, 2007, he is batting .457; he is living and hoping to make it from Harlem to the major leagues

Comments On April 3, 2020, About the Economics of Our Communities

Maurice G Faucette

The Black Community must get out of the "Convenience Economy" into a "Survival Economy" and then into a "Prosperity Economy".

Remember the person who bought their lunch every day. Sometimes, it was just a can of tuna and crackers. (Many spend $5-10 every day for lunch) I "betcha" She is not living paycheck to paycheck. The Black Community must get out of the "Convenience Economy" into a "Survival Economy" and then into a "Prosperity Economy".

Despite Billions being pumped into the inner city to renovate and build buildings, Most Black inner cities are still stuck in a "Welfare Economy," as are most Black Communities of Color. The. money does not circulate. One trip in and one trip out! In fact, under the "Smoke and Mirrors Community Development Gentrification Economy," the money does not even make a trip in. A builder in Queens sends a Check to a Supplier in Brooklyn. The supplies get delivered to the Black Community, and the building gets "Rehabbed" with the Minister's Name on it. The workers come in from everywhere but the community and spend, little money while there. Their direct deposit paycheck goes back to where They came from... Many do buy lunch and drinks from the local Bodega's...Then, many want to know why our people are like They are.

Yes, I studied all this in school. As Minister Louis Farrakhan said, "If you could take back home what you learned in corporate America, you could **almost Free Our People overnight".** He did also say you would be resented. I will go to my grave knowing I tried to wake my people up! You can lead a horse to water, but you cannot make Him drink!

I wrote this on April 9, 2020. You can see I do not like the welfare mentality of many in the Black Community, as everything has to go through the "Buffer" class. My comments...

My Leadership Paradigm has always been no matter who is complicit with the problems in our community. We must do for ourselves. Why is diabetes high in lower-income communities? This is attributed to the eating of processed foods. Why are asthma rates higher? Yes, Our people have been sold out a long time ago by "Bougie Niggers", who have been the White Man Powers that be lackeys. These medical institutions in low-income people of color neighborhoods have been bringing in all these profit-making medications and experiments.

Yet "We must do for Self". We must change our behavior.

We must make Babies we can take care of. The Government is not giving WIC, Welfare, Section 8, or SNAP to help you. They give you enough so that your inner drive for Liberation will not flourish and cause you to **Liberate Yourself**.

(I need a beat for My Corona Virus Rap Song! Anybody got one?)

During the corona virus back in March, there were complaints on the news that because the schools were closed, many children had nothing to eat. Please forgive the profanity, but this is the way my mother spoke, about free food.

I can hear my mother now saying, “Fuck a Free Meal”. You want something to eat, bring your ass in the house” “I work too God Damn hard for my children to be depending on the Mother Fucking Welfare to Feed My Children” That is for them Mother Fuckers sitting on a garbage can all day waiting on a Welfare Check”.... if you think I am making this up, you better ask somebody! Dorothy Mae Mosley Faucette, I appreciate you more and more every day!

3/20/20 Comments on the Corona Virus

Maurice G. Faucette

If Your definition of War is tanks and planes, U R an inside-the-box thinker.

The ultimate Samurai is taught that you will do everything possible to defeat Your enemy without pulling Your Sword from Your sheath, outside the box thinking.

The Japanese started an economic War with America in the 1980s when President Bush went over there with a hat in hand and choked on a chicken bone.

Malcolm once said that “the Best slave is one who does not know He/She is a slave”. The best opponent is one who does not know He/She is in a fight.!. This Virus is an attempt to bring the World to its Knees!

Mitt, Julius Caesar and the Godfather

Maurice G. Faucette

Mitt smelled the blood in the water, aka a shot at the Presidency, and took it! Yet, at the moment of truth 2, Publicans bailed on Him! Now, I do not know if a horse head was on their bed, or if a million was in their account, or maybe a burnt body on the grave on the grave of someone close to them. Did they not do this to Ted to tell him not to run? (Yes, a burnt body was found on JFK's grave years ago, and you can Google it!)

Or are Dr Umar's comments about the plane crash true? Did not an episode of "24" when the Black Senator was running for President and a lot of people lost their lives to cover the identity of the assassin sent to terminate the Black Senator? Perhaps They were warned not to ride "Copters"! Now Mitt kicked out of CPAC! At least Mitt did not get the same sentence as Tessio when he plotted against the King.

I Want Players Who Really Want to Play for Me

Maurice G. Faucette

No, I never Coached on the Pro level, but I 1st Coached at age 14! I won My 1st Championship at 15! My #1 requirement as a Coach is that U really have to want to Play for Me!

My Coaching Experience and My career in Corporate America, My 3 Terms as President of a Xerox Black Caucus Group. We fought for the rights of Black People for Corporate upward mobility. I had my own career de-railed because of my outspokenness. I have concluded from everything I read, heard on the radio, watched on TV this weekend, and understood the "Unwritten" rules of getting s job. I have concluded COLIN KAPERNICK does not want to play! (lol)

When People want to play or are willing to fight they have to be respected. A wise man like Xerox CEO David Kearns, when faced with a fight in the 1970's from organized black employees for upward mobility, took a radical position. David Kearns took this energy and give the black employees the opportunity to advance.! He opened up the doors for Black Upward mobility at Xerox! It is a documentary case study at Harvard Business School! Yet some of us who were outspoken still got our careers de-railed! Some of us were even held back and **sold out by Our Own People!**

Be Careful When Elevating an Issue!

Maurice G. Faucette

Whenever you elevate an issue, in my opinion, make sure you have documented evidence.

Any time you challenge authority or Power, You have to prepare yourself for the repercussions. Only you can make that decision in regards to what price you are willing to pay.

You have to utilize the principles of both Conventional and Guerrilla warfare. The Book "The Art of War" will give you philosophical anecdotes.

May Be Unto You!

Best Enemy

Maurice G. Faucette

When the masses are enslaved inside the box, anyone who presents outside-the-box rationale is labeled Crazy. Malcolm X said, "The best slave is one who does not know he is a slave." The Masses are in Slavery. The best enemy in a War is one who does not he is in a War. Why tanks and planes? "Rona Virus" has done more to weaken the economy than any war. In fact, a war economy saved America after the depression.

Starting the Journey to Understand Black Males

Maurice G. Faucette

To understand the problems with young black males, 1st understand the concepts of Maslow's Hierarchy of Needs in Psychology 101. Then, relate it to this, many black males never live at an address that has their name on it. They live in their Mamma, Grand Mamma, Auntie, Nana, Girl Friend, Baby Mamma Apt... #1 Step in being a man is being self-sufficient.

God Bless the Child That has their own....

Ramblings

Maurice G. Faucette

The illogical world events are too logical.

I have studied boom-bust economies and Keynesian Economic Theory along with the principles of Power and Oppression. I could write an essay or book on it but only 1-2 would read.

Our People are following Our so-called Leaders down a path of destruction. Malcolm tried to wake The Black Man up, but petty, jealousies and individual selfish missions were put above the People. May Peace Be Unto You?

I just got a new TV service along with Netflix; I am minimizing My FB time. I may write in the middle of the night, but then I am off until after 8 PM. I am going to watch the NFL Draft, the documentary about the Malcolm X Assassination and the Irishman, the order of which I do not know!.....

The Man, the Legend, the Myth, but Definitely the Truth about Jesus

Maurice G. Faucette

Fact: There was a Man named Jesus. He was born to Mary, A Man named Joseph raised him as his Son! Joseph and Mary reportedly told people he was conceived through the **"Immaculate Conception".** Many laughed at them! Some believed he was the Son of God; Many did not, depending on how you defined the Son of God! Many in Power, just like The Democrats and Republicans, feared Jesus. They feared that the belief by the People that Jesus was the "New King" could overthrow Their Balance of Power, It did not matter whether he was indeed the Son of God or not!

So **Powerful** was this belief that a "King" who was the Son of God, whether true or not, that in the spirit of "The Prince." written by Nikolai Machiavelli, that **"if the Baby in the Crib is a threat to your Power then kill the Baby in the crib..** King Herod sent his men to find baby Jesus and stick a sword in his heart! Now, at this point, it mattered little to some of these men that Jesus was the Son of God. It mattered little that he was born via his mother not having intercourse with anyone. Which matters is that many believe this is TRUE. In most, it inspires good feelings and belief that people who do believe in the legend do great deeds. It does not matter whether it is fact, fiction or a combination of both, People do great things beyond what is scientifically and humanly possible! That is a fact.

Feeding the Hungry

Please give me a comprehensive profile of who is going to bed hungry in New York City. I ask because we need to fix the problem. I heard on the news that 1 in 5 children in NYC went to bed hungry, or they got some new term...

With SNAP, all the Food Pantries, and organizations giving out free food, please give me a profile on the family where a child went to bed hungry. Before the "playa haters" come after the messenger, my question is the profile of the family and why are not these programs reaching these children! In New York, with Democrats running things at all levels of “government” and based on there being enough food on the face of the earth to feed everyone, why are people in New York going to bed hungry?

Yes, food is destroyed and sometimes not planted with programs passed by Congress. Programs like Federal Price Support Programs. I studied it in school. Now, just give me the profile!

I want to understand the profile and start to fix it. I am a get-it-done person. So save all the rhetoric and BS and give me the profile.

Now, just give me the profile! Let us make sure everyone is fed.

Why Cannot Our Children Read?

In response to a post that after the 3rd grade, only 30% of our children are reading at a 3rd-grade level.

Where are you getting the stats about our kids and the 3rd-grade reading level? I totally disagree. It is the responsibility of the Parents to ensure their kids get educated. If the schools are doing such a poor job, why are the PTA meetings not crowded? We do not have 100% participation at Parent Teacher Conferences.

Why are school board elections in many communities almost ignored? Schools get more "Gument" money for failing than succeeding.

The numbers you give need to be thoroughly "vetted". Our kids, and I mean Black Children, are doing better than what some report. If the Schools are failing our kids, as you say, then the Parents need to challenge the Board of Education like My Mother did at PS 184 in South Harlem in the 1950s.

I fought the corrupt school board 5 in Central Harlem, and I never thought I would be fighting Black People to educate our kids. This is the same fight that my mother fought the Jews who ran and, to this day, pretty much run the Board of Education in NY.

As long as the Black Community stays in the victimization

Mentality, we will get the short end of the stick. If the schools are as bad as you say, then the parents need to knock the doors down.

Why have they not?

Americans 1st

If we were Americans 1st every day, most of the problems would disappear. Power thrives on division and manipulation. Those who understand this know that if all people of color were to leave, America would still be divided. **An "All White Nation" would not exist, upon all the non whites leaving.** The "All White." America would revert back to its European divisions,. I do not know which of the "White" groups would catch hell 1st. I suspect it would be the Italians or Irish, or maybe the Poles or Jews. Take your pick.

Until we heal the hate in the hearts of humans, we are doomed to the same scenario.

Black FBI Agents Discrimination Litigation

Black FBI Agents feel the Agency discriminates against them! We felt the same way At XEROX, and wc did something about it! Starting back in the 1970's! I am proud of the 3 terms I served as President of the Northeast Region (Black) Caucus Group MAME aka Metropolitan Area Minority Employees.

It started out as the Black Caucus under the late Art Crawford and was changed to MAME under David C Smith to include other minorities....In my opinion, we should have left it as the Black Caucus because, with the exception of a few, not everyone wants to help prepare the meal but wants a seat at the table when it is time to eat! Yeah, I said it!

.

Subconscious Patterns in Choosing a Relationship

I may be wrong! Out of the males who approach her, if a female constantly selects males who mistreat her, then she may want to look at how she decides who to be with.

The female, as to who to allow in her life in a free society, **always makes the final decision about who she is going to be with.**

Males may approach her and ask her out, but it is her decision. If she keeps making bad decisions, whose fault is that? Please note my use of female/male and not Woman and Man. The 1st is a matter of biology, the latter, well, if I have to explain, that may be the problem....,

Was Trump's Walter Reed Visit for Show or Treatment?

Trust me, the White House has everything that Walter Reed has. The Medical Facility there is second to none. That move today was as much political as it is medical. They have it above ground, and they have it in the bunker underground, and they got it out west in NORAD, and they got it in the UN and Pentagon and s few other secret locations.

Like Hyman Roth said, “Fly My Doctor in from Miami” that is what the rich and powerful do. Vito Corleone went home from the Hospital when most could not... lol!

Housing Projects to Condominiums?

If I had been Congressman...

King Towers has a projected rent roll of $84,000,000 annually. Real Estate investors multiply that by the area average for value. Using a different 8 to 12 times multiple King Towers is guesstimated @ $650 million to a Billion after renovation. This is based on 2000 apartments with an average rent of $3500. Then, HDFC apartments close by. that people got from the city for $250 are selling for close to a Million, and larger apartments over a Million.

What would an investor pay per unit for 2000 units with a potential market value of $2 Billion plus within 5 years? **That is why the tenants should organize and go to their Congressman Espilliat and get a Federal buyout for King Towers and convert King Towers to Condos.** This way, tenants so they can reap the benefits of gentrification. The subsidy to buy out for the tenants would be based on the number of years renting. Those who have been there since opening should get theirs for $1.

Please do not tell me it cannot be done because HPD did it right across the street and the tenants got the apartments for $250.00. Some are now selling HDFC Co-ops that they bought from the city for $250.00 within 5 blocks of King Towers for over a $1,000,000.00

Louis Farrakhan asked if we could take what we learned in Corporate America back home. He said we could free our people overnight. He also said those with the knowledge would be resented... He said this in a speech he did in 1980 speech he did in 1980 to Black Corporate Managers of Xerox, IBM and AT&T. He also said there would never be a 2nd meeting because it was too powerful and the powers that be would not allow it.

There has never been a 2nd meeting.

Learned Behavior

When you get into the psychology of learned behavior, you may question everything we have ever been taught. I am not passing judgment because any judgment is based on what I was taught since birth. What is considered decency is not absolute and is not innate behavior. It is a learned behavior, just like racism. You are not born with it, you are taught it.

Books like "1984" try to get us to delve into both learned and innate behavior. Those who benefit from it try and dictate and control it. This is the behavior of "Gument" and the Media! They want you to think a certain way so as to control you. **They program you by talking to you on a grade school level.** They do not want you to think. They just want you to react.

Watch! The comments will deal with the specifics and not the concepts of learned versus innate behavior!

Media Depiction of Trump on a Grade-School Mentality

You may or may not like Donald Trump! Yet do not let the media talk to u on a grade school level about his business. A billion in debt does not define anyone as successful or unsuccessful.

WHAT is their NET WORTH is the key? Is the debt constructive or destructive?

In general, borrowing to buy property is constructive, while borrowing to take a vacation is generally destructive.

Forbes: "It is important to note, as Trump did Thursday night, that he also has significant assets. Forbes values them at $3.66 billion, enough to make his net worth an estimated $2.5 billion. He is not broke, despite what many critics and the talking down to you on a grade school level media want you to believe.

.

Why I Say Trump Is a Racist

I was asked why I feel Donald Trump is a racist. Before you give me your 4th-grade ignorant answer, I thought about it. I asked myself as if this was a college essay to outline facts and separate them from opinion. Unless you can take a high lighter and outline it as fact, do not say it!

Then, from a point of conjecture, if he is or not, what is your benefit or fear if he is or isn't. Since I am not in school and, I am not being graded and I am doing this within 15 minutes, does it really matter if I am right it not, or factually accurate??? Here it goes!

My gut feeling is that he is. He discriminated against Black people in renting. His businesses appear to not be well represented with Black people. He appears to be supportive of groups that have exhibited anti-black behavior. Now, with that being said, I, Maurice Faucette, believe this Man is a racist. As a result, I do not trust him to be President of the United States. In a second term, he does not have to answer to America because he is not up for re-election. I do not trust him to be President when he can get the Senate, Congress and the Supreme Court to do his bidding. I do not trust his interpretation of the Bible or that of the Constituency that supports him. I do not trust this Man with unchecked Power.

I have considered going to 3rd party, but my mission is to stop Trump. You have to survive the heart attack to fight the cancer.

For the record, before the Democrats start sticking their chests out. I have Democratic representation at every level of Government except the Presidency. They are arrogant think they are better than the masses elitists.

The present state of NY is the Democrats fault. But Donald Trump is a racist, and he represents racists. I am not so much voting for Biden but against Trump. He and all the Bible thumpers can thump that Bible just like the slave masters did. **NYC will get worse under an all-Democratic regime,** but Trump unchecked, with the Senate, Congress and Court behind him, is a dangerous Man.

I have considered going to 3rd party, but my mission is to stop Trump. You have to survive the heart attack to fight the cancer. America is stuck between a rock and a hard place.

Since it looks like Trump may be President, we have to find a way to make it work for Black America! Maybe I am wrong about Trump! Maybe the challenge will be like the furnace that melts the impurities to make pure gold.

Dow Jones and the Presidency

(2000}

Dow down almost a Grand! I said if it hit 30,000, "Frump" would be re-elected! Almost 0 chance of that happening. New York Biden/Harris all the way. Not enough upstate /Long Island Republican votes to balance out City.

The Bigot in the White House may have awakened the "Sleeping Giant" of American Politics, the "Black Vote."

But Electoral Votes still the rule of the day. Trump still has a chance. **The Black vote must overwhelm those "Swing or Battleground" States!**

Now, if we can get the Black Politicians off their knees, kissing the parties behind and start answering to the working class of the masses, maybe we can make change.

Turn all these Homeless Shelters into work camps. Get these Streets Cleaned up and No Graffiti in NYC! Subsidized Housing focusing on giving jobs to those who will live in them and not the profit motive of the developers!

Real Change is needed!

.

Political Peace of Mind

I have found peace of mind by not listening to irrational, illogical thoughts. The media talks to us on a grade-school level. I understand why a lot of people support Trump, but I do not spend my time worrying about it! **He is proud to be White and has represented White America with no apologies.** I personally think the **Democrats are elitist, arrogant, condescending** think they are better than the masses. I voted against Trump because he is a racist. So Joe and Kamala got my vote.

There are racists in both parties. The "Racists" are just easier to find in the Republican Party!

My loss of Faith in the New York Democrats

If you want to see why I have lost faith in the New York

Democrats. Come to the Wakefield section of the North Bronx. The North Bronx has Democratic representation at every level of Government, including the Presidency.

In the North Bronx, particularly the Wakefield section, you will see how this Democratic "do goody", feel sorry for everybody attitude has messed up this neighborhood. 3 Homeless shelters within blocks of each other. The streets are filthy. Graffiti has returned. The males from the homeless shelters panhandle on the street and use the gas station of Nereid and Carpenter as a park. Writing letters, going o meetings is a waste of time. The politicians pontificate and promise, but nothing gets done. But come election time, the robocalls will come one after the other. Your mailbox will be stuffed with literature, but nothing gets done.

. **Maybe if the King of the Democrats, Barrack Obama, comes to Wakefield, the streets will be cleaned for his visit. I am sure the New York Democrats do not want the King to see their failures.**

Have I Made The Best Use Of My God-Given Talents?

Sometimes, I doubt myself as to whether I have used God's gifts wisely, like now, early before sunrise!

Yet, when I think of what we were able to accomplish on 115th, building not so much a baseball field from a garbage dump but an oasis where our children could breathe and dream. A field here we could mold them to focus on an objective to some thought was preparation to win a game, but more importantly, preparation for life.

To battle when you are down like we did in Cooperstown, down 8-4 in the last inning of the playoff in the last inning to come back and win 9-8. Or to be behind against the Harlem LL, down 4 with 2 outs and nobody on to come back and win. To tackle 2 seemingly invincible foes, like beating the Young Devils in 1967 to win the Championship and the Undefeated OLS Knights with now MLB pitcher 6'1" 12-year-old Dellin Betances 20 years ago.

I tried my best to teach you to battle to prepare to believe in myself and to make your Mother proud of you.

Go to school and get an education.

I walked away from any shot at a political career and basically corporate America to do what I loved to do, something I started, being chosen by God at age 14 to do. No guidebook, no mentor, just faith in what I could do. There was always some divine guidance. The proof is in the pudding. I have had some conversations verbal and texting recently with former players that have made me feel good reflecting on what I taught them, Isaiah. Keith Mazyck, Sidney Herbert, Danny Myers, James Faust, and Alex DaGreat.

Spiritual signs like August 31, 1997, when America's Queen, my Sister Regina Abdul Salam, aka Pat, was called Home by the Lord. Pee Wee Day was scheduled that day, and we held it. We held a Home Run Derby that day for the Pee Wees, the kids 10 and under!

We put up cones that day as the fences were too far. That day, all the Pee Wees that went to bat, and only one Home Run was hit!

As I left the field that day with My 2 Nephews, Ayinde and Rasheed, who had lost their Mother hours earlier that day, to take them to be with "Family",as their real family was at the field they played, on I glanced back to see Coach Elsa Lopez getting everybody in a circle to hold hands to Pray for us.

It is 26 years later, and both are Men now. Ayinde works in the Cable field, and Rasheed, who I believe I remember pointing to the sky 26 years ago at the age of 9, being the only one to hit a Home

Run that day, as he dedicated it to his Mother in Heaven, is Teacher now with a Masters Degree!

God is Great!

All White Church

I see where a church in Minnesota was permitted to be **"Whites" only!** See how that works out if they are asked to define "White"! Mmmmmmmmmmm !

.

Pricing Theory and Perception

You think these name brand luxury products are worth all the money. **$300.00 sneakers, $2,000.00 handbags?** Pricing theory and building a mystique about a product is a PHD level study into the psychology of the human mind. People are paid and make millions by studying us and selling us what we are gullible for.

No need for chains when you can enslave a people through deception and their own ignorance.

Focus on Self

If you have achieved wealth and/or success through your brain, You can only pull 1 or 2 people up because the rest are too busy listening to the BS they are saying bout you!

Celebrity Politicians

Black people have made politicians celebrities!

Vito Corleone carried them like coins in his pocket!

Present a bill for services!

They are **OUR** Servants!

A Drug Named of Power

More Intoxicating than

Heroin,

Cocaine,

Sex,

Nicotine,

Food!

POWER!

•

R Kelly School of "Pimping".

Yeah, I watched the R Kelly documentary... I thought it was a documentary on how to be a Pimp, and probably a lot of young guys were taking notes.

This pimp, though, was rich, so he did not need to pimp for money. He pimped because he liked it. By the way, the rhetoric says we look down on Pimps. Malcolm X said to judge people by their conscious behavior. What does the overall behavior of the black community say about pimping? Do our actions say we blast it or idolize it? Keep your females close.

This documentary educated a lot of vultures on how vulnerable our females are and how to lure them in and use them.

Do We Really Live in a 2 Party System?

Do we live in a 2 Party system? It is just an illusion. It is like Wrestling, where the mission is to get paid by putting on a scripted conflict!

Both the Democrats and Republicans are self-serving elitists intent on making themselves rich and above the people expecting to be idolized and worshiped. They point fingers at each other and appear to be arguing while enjoying lobster dinners with champagne toasts.

They pass so-called laws that send everything through the "buffer class". The "buffer class" class has to get their cut before the crumbs trickle down to the masses. **In the Black Communities where people of color live, the streets are dirty, crime is out of control, and the social programs which employ the "buffer class" at exorbitant salaries to fix poverty while the impoverished make no progress.**

They play the game of blaming each other so as to never have the blame placed at their feet collectively.

. No, this is not a sideline observation. If you want to see my collection of letters to the powers that be, whether they be Presidents or local officials, just ask. White or Black, or if they are simply People of color, with a select few, they ignore the people's need for true leadership. When true leadership comes to threaten them, the bag of dirty tricks to smear and stop them is endless!

America is in trouble! Adolph Hitler sneaked up on Germany and the world by 1st leading Germany to economic prosperity. The Germans world wide respected image in the 1930's lead to great self-esteem. A totalitarian type of government may seem far away at this time. Yet history does not stop today. With modern advances in technology that Orwell could not fathom when "1984" was written, w**e stand in the threat of "Big Brother".**

It does not matter whether led by Biden or Trump, the threat of the government totally dominating our lives causes concern.

The real day will come when one who looks like you is chosen to lead, only to perhaps find out they are not one of you! Mark my words! Store this away. Be careful what you ask for...

The Mirror of the Economically Oppressed

Someone asked how can the elite make so much money while the masses suffer...my response............they control access to knowledge by owning all the vehicles to distribute such. Those in the lower economic groups deal with pettiness, like who is the G.O.A.T in basketball, aka Greatest of All Time, Lower-income people can be incented into paying $250 for a pair of sneakers that cost a fraction to make. They are made overseas, and the economy where the lower economic groups live get little or no economic benefit from this sneaker wealth...You do not have to steal from a community if they are fighting to give it to the wealthy. You can deceive a million people with a pair of sneakers but only rob one at a time with a gun...

Where Do I Go from Here?

I could pack up things in My Lincoln, ship or sell the furniture, cut off the news stations, put on Sirius or Pandora, go out to My crib in New Mexico, reduce my cost of living, not have to deal with all this nastiness in NYC. A city where people have no respect for each other. Cars are racing through the streets like the Indy 500. Fireworks are out of control where people of color live. All these fireworks, even though we are supposed to be **broke.**

The Black Communities, The streets are filthy, the street baskets are overflowing, where Homeless shelters are being dumped, where politicians ignore my letters...... Maybe go teach at an HBCU, aka Historically Black College or University, and buy me a nice home in the Bougie Niggas part of town. (Every big Black Southern town got one) get an **Escalade**, and talk in theory about the problems in Black America while living with the Bougie Niggas in their part of town, Mmmm, but I am from 115th Street!!!

I hope many Baby Daddies watched the NBA draft. It was a salute to Black Fatherhood, Ja Morant, RJ Barrett and Coby White. Coby lost his father 2 years ago to liver cancer. Baby Daddies, not present in your child's life, like the fathers of these 3 players, have you ever wondered how much more your children could have been had you been there? I am not just talking physically but financially, morally, and spiritually. What more could your child have accomplished if you had been there like their dads? If you have put in the time, like their Dads.

Liberation Finance

Over 40 years ago at Xerox, a rookie salesperson like me, told me he went to pick up a classmate. The home was beautiful, and he told the classmate's father how nice it was. The father told him, I do not own this home! I own an identical home across the street. My brother lives in it! He said, "My brother owns this home."

I never forgot that story. Stop listening to the media talking to you on a grade school level and get knowledge!

I do not teach personal finance and budgeting! Liberate your mind!

There is more than one way to skin a cat.

Perry Jr.

Perry Jr was killed not because He was An Ex-Offender but because He was Black, and Officer Chauven has some subconscious,

Freudian phallic insecurity issues as the truth comes out about Chauvin knowing “George the Landlord” and His association with White Women at the Club They both worked at!

The Family did not call him George Floyd. They called him Perry Jr. Where was Perry Senior?

A Revolutionary Basketball Strategy

In a playoff game the Phoenix Suns scored the game winning basket with..... .8 seconds remaining. This was done on an in bounds pass under the basket. In my opinion, Boogie Cousins, the Clippers defender, was out of position. He should have been standing in between the out of bounds passer, and the basket. He needed to make sure that the ball went way back to the back court or on the side. The Suns then would have..8 seconds to get off a long distance catch and shoot shot to possibly win the game. I like those odds better for the defense.

Now, with all that being said, most coaches deal with things on inside the inside-the-box basis. Over a period of time, tactics and strategies evolve. **A fan like me can have an idea, but the odds of getting it in the hands of a college or professional coach are almost zero.**

Back in the 1950s, a Security Guard at Yankee Stadium was able to put in place a revolutionary concept that changed Pro Football. It is so commonplace today that you will not believe that this Security Guard was the one to design it. Yet it is true.

Let me take you back to the mid-1950s and professional football when an outside box stinker did something that no other NFL team had ever did at that time. If you see old game films of the NFL before this play, you'll see that the quarterback always had two running backs to protect him. Three receivers went out on the platy. All teams were inside-the-box thinkers.

Nobody varied from this. In the mid-1950s, a security guard at Yankee Stadium wrote up a play called the "home run play".. It found its way into his hands into the Giants coaching staff. . **Today, the chance of a fan or security guard getting anything into the hands of an NFL, NBA, NHL, NCAA or MLB coach is very difficult, if not almost impossible.**

Back in the 1950s, security guard wrote out a "home run" play. Now, what is the "home run" play? What does it have to do with the Phoenix Suns and Los Angeles Clippers? Let us look at the Home Run play. Up to that point, the defenses only prepared to cover 3 receivers. Up to that point only three receivers were sent out. The security guard designed a play to send 5 fast receivers out. Figuring that the defenses would not be prepared for 5 fast receivers, he figured he could isolate a fast receiver on a slow linebacker. This was usually the case at that time. Linebackers were built differently in the 1950's. To take advantage, the New York Giants actually bought in two defensive backs as receivers. They bought in Erich Barnes and Jimmy Patton. The New York Giants scored a touchdown.

Since the game was taped. All NFL teams were able to study this play. They made adjustments. They were prepared the next time someone sent 5 receivers out, which is now inside-the-box thinking.

Outside-the-box thinking usually becomes inside-the-box thinking.

The Giants caught their opponents with their pants down. Once again, what does that have to do with the Phoenix Suns and the Los Angeles Clippers? For the record, **I called Monty Williams, offering him a new strategy to defend an out-of-bounds play.** I have not checked the NBA or NCAA rules. Maybe what I am proposing is illegal. You research it for me. **I also went over to the Pit in Albuquerque, New Mexico, looking for Coach Pitino.** I left a note on his assistant's car, and I left a message. I got no response.

Let's review. Boogie Cousins should have positioned himself so as to make sure there was no pass straight to the basket. I am gonna give you a revolutionary strategy right now for that situation.. As far as I know, there's no rule against it, and while I may have seen it once, I never saw it again. Everybody just does it the same old way with one defender..

If I am in that situation I need to guarantee that they will be no pass straight to the basket. In a situation like this I am putting two people on the ball on the out-of-bounds play. I'm gonna make it so that they cannot get the ball in bounds without throwing a deep loop pass out near the half-court or into the back court. My other 3 defenders will have time to react and to defend the shot. Best case, the offense will have to make a long shot to win.

The offense can try to pass between my defender's legs. We have to be prepared and alert for this.

Sometimes you can't see the forest for the trees. Now I called Monty Williams. I don't get a return phone call. I left a Coach Pitino of the University of New Mexico Lobos to call me. No response from the Lobos. They probably think I'm some type of nut or something. Not that I'm gonna change my attention to baseball and what they need to do to fix their problems.

NBA Not Far Moved from Wrestling?

NBA is one step removed from Wrestling! My Man says he stopped watching when they rigged the draft, so the NY got Ewing! It was one of the drugs, I believe, that was listed on a wall in Fulton Street, along with comic books, sneakers, anything to keep the Black Man's focus on cleaning up his community, taking care of his children and liberating our minds!

Their Time. Their Way

For those who criticize the tactics and strategies of the Black Lives Matters Movement. The mission is to get the job done! We had our time, and we did it our way based on the resources and technology we had at that time.

To those out there doing their thing, it is Your time! Your way! For those who are out there now, who criticize the generations before them, do not underestimate what generations before you have done.

We did not even have beepers yet, less more cell phones with high-def cameras. We had 3 TV stations that went off at night, less more than 300-400 around-the-clock stations.

The Black Radio station was all the way down at the end of the dial. Many times, You could not get it. Our social media was standing on the corner. We had one or 1- 2 Black Reporters who had their hands tied and their mouths gagged.

We had more than our fair share of Uncle Tom and Aunt Thomasinas. The battle plan sometimes was in the hands of the oppressor before the strategy meeting ended.

I salute your Courage, Bravado, and Spirit de Corps. Your Time! Your way! Get the job done. Some of us will cut bait while you fish. Your time! Your way!

Bring home the bacon!

Snatching Victory from Defeat!

I dedicate this to Larry Clark & Nathaniel "Peppy" Topping. Why? Because neither wanted to give the basketball ball up in a game! Sometimes, players who would not pass were called Jerry Butler after the soul singer for his hit song "Never Gonna Give You Up." While he meant the girl, we meant the ball!

When We played the Jersey Stars in Sucker up at Hickman Park in upper Manhattan. I was a Player/Coach. We played with 3 Guards. James Faust, aka Jimmy "The Distributor". Jimmy had to keep the peace between Larry and "Peppy. Even though they had been teammates on the South Harlem Reds years earlier, these two spent the 1st 21 1/2 minutes of the game fighting over the ball. They were arguing like they were back in the Big Park, on 114th and Lenox, aka Malcolm X Blvd. All this time, we were getting beat.

As I have told the story many times, We were down by 16 points with 8:30 minutes left to play! A lead, while not insurmountable, is tough to overcome, even when a team is playing together. Two players were playing selfish individual basketball. We were not playing together as a team. We were on our way to getting beat.

Then the Jersey Stars, a team of college players, made a big mistake., The Jersey Stars started laughing at and taunting us. One thing I was taught is to never embarrass, humiliate or taunt your opponent. They started doing all types of Toma-Hawk, Slam Dunks and pointing and laughing at us. I called a time-out. We were down with down 16 points with 8 minutes and 30 seconds to play. My team was mad. The two maddest were Larry "LC" Clark and Nathaniel "Peppy" Topping!

Both had basketball credentials. the Jersey Stars did not know about. Larry starred at Hanover and then went to Dartmouth to play basketball. Peppy had played for two legendary high school programs, Rice n Harlem and Dunbar in Baltimore. They were both in their mid-20s and while they could still play. They were in weekend playground condition, not in top all-year-round condition.

They were seething along with Jimmy Faust, Danny Meyers, Doug Murphy, and Jimmy King. I asked them one question, "Do you want to win this game? To a Man, they all said yes. I told them that if they did what I told them to do, they would win! They said, "OK" Larry and Peppy put that petty Bull Shit apart.

They both came up under me playing for the South Harlem Reds. They know I am 200% about winning. I have won in all 3 Sports as a player and as a Coach. We came back from 16 down with 8 ½ minutes to play.

I played about 30 seconds, and I was called for an offensive foul and I retired from Harlem Summer Basketball. (I was actually tripped). Wow, We have some Memories! We are from The Big

Park Where “Champions” were Made.

The memories from that game and others are why I thought the Patriots could come back against the Falcons. I have been feeling great since the Patriots won. I never doubted them, and I never fully understood why until tonight while riding home and remembering our victory over the Jersey Stars, along with other come-from-behind victories or going up against great odds and winning…

My competitiveness, intensity and heart have never been questioned in Baseball, Basketball or football. Teams are an extension of the Coach...the Patriots' Victory brought back so many memories of times when teams I have been involved with snatched Victory from Defeat... Like the aforementioned victory over the much bigger Jersey Stars from Newark, all D-1 ballplayers averaging over 6'8" on the front line, and our tallest player was Doug Murphy @ 6'4" tall.

I know how the Patriots felt, as I have been involved multiple times…

We were down to our last out with nobody on vs. The Harlem Little League 19u Team that was leading us by 6 runs in the last inning. My 1st 2 hitters did not follow directions, and we were down to our last out. Down to our last out, nobody on base, down by 6 runs. The chances of us winning were astronomical.,...I was mad and told my team if they did what I told them to do we would win.

Yes, it does sound familiar. My 2 Power hitters, Bryan "Big Bang" Howard and Latif "Kid-Diddy" Abdul Salam Faucette, both battled and got on base.

As part of my mental training of my players I used to ask my players about the different ways to get on base. I also asked a trick question: "How many hits can a team get without scoring a run?" The answer is 6. The purpose is to make players think. At the moment of truth, you must have every tool in your toolbox ready.

We were ready... Batter by batter, we got on base. Your job is to get on base by any of the means we reviewed. Pass it to the next batter. ... .Do not try to be a hero. Just do your job. Eventually, we got the bases loaded.

Then, the moment of truth. We were within one swing distance.

One swing distance is when with one swing, you can win or tie a game. Robert Knights came to bat. We were within one swing distance. I told him that we were on a take-two diet. A take-two diet is when your team is behind, and very few outs are left. In other words, do not swing the bat until you have 2 strikes. You do this when pitchers is wild and have a hard time throwing strikes.

They walk a lot of batters.

The Harlem LL, though, had just switched pitchers. My

Coaching experience told me that a new pitcher usually throws a fastball right down the middle. It takes a disciplined, focused hitter to take advantage of this. I told Robert Knights not to take the bat off his shoulder unless the pitch was perfect. In other words, it had to be exactly in his sweet spot. Robert Knights was disciplined and focused, the son of an NYPD Detective Squad leader. He knew how to take directions and execute them. What happened next was unbelievable. The first pitch was a fastball right down the middle. Robert Knights took that bat off his shoulder. A Grand Slam by Robert Knight., to whom I told that bat had not better leave his bat on a 0-0 count unless it was out of here, and it was out of here...Final score: South Harlem Reds 12, Harlem LL 11... We snatched Victory from Defeat!

Baseball fan Dellin Betances of the NY Yankees, now the NY Mets, is an MLB All-Star. In 2000, he was a 6'1" 12-year-old pitching for the OLS Mets. When the OLS Mets came to our field on 115th Street and pitched. He scared the S__T out of my kids. He threw very hard, and his stature as a 12-year-old 6'1" pitcher intimidated my kids. He struck out 17 of 18 batters, but our motto is, "OK, you may beat us in April, but can you beat us in August?" We put our players through the meat grinder. We put them in the Caribe League against big, strong Dominican kids who received top-notch coaching from former MLB and Minor League Players. My Coaches even speculated that some of the kids were over-aged. I told my coaches that unless they were going to protest before the game, they would leave it alone. We do not want our players to have excuses. We worked hard to get better. If we got beat, I would tell our kids, "We take our ass whooping like a man. A man makes no excuses. A man goes back to the drawing board and works hard so he will not get beat again.

August came. We had played 80 games by then. In Cooperstown Baseball World, as the guest of the late "Eddie Einhorn," one of the owners of the Chicago White Sox, We faced 2 of the best 12u Teams to be found. We faced the Bay Men of Long Island and the Phoenix Yankees. No, we did not beat them, but we were competitive. You must teach your players to be competitive. Then, you can cut down on errors, both mental and physical. Winning is all about total concentration and focus. We were focused and ready for the OLS Mets and Dellin Betances.

Game 1 Champion Series South Harlem Reds 4 and OLS Mets 1. We beat Betances. Troy Andrews totally out pitched Betances.

Game 2 We fought back from a 6-run deficit in game 2 to tie the game on a Grand Slam by Troy Andrews. We lost 7-6 after they scored.

Game 3, The Championship on the line. We started Troy Andrews, but the OLS Mets did not start Betances. Betances played

Center Field. Late in the game, we were up 2. We had the runners 2nd and 3rd. A hit here, and the OLS Mets were about done. Ray Maldonado, the Coach of the OLS Mets, walked to the mound. He summoned Betances to come in from the outfield and pitch. Ray Maldonado knew the Championship was on the line. We were at the moment of truth. He bought Betances to stop us. Juan Cruz was the batter. As he went to the plate, I told him to dig a hole in the dirt with his foot. This is a psychological ploy to let the pitcher know you are ready. You have to let a "flame thrower" know you are not intimidated. Yes, we were intimidated in April, but now it is m May. It was a monumental battle. Betances threw heat on every pitch. Juan Cruz, with his Mother and Father in attendance, kept fouling pitches off. Then, the hardest pitch of the game, the moment of truth, Juan swung. It was a line drive single up the middle. We took their heart with that hit. We increased the lead to 4! We won! Were were OLS Champions! For the record, it was the 1st of four in a row!

Back in the 1960s, For 2 years, we could not beat the Young Devils. They were from Taft Projects, and most of our kids were from King Towers. Several had tried out for the Young Devils and been cut. (A member of the 1966 Young Devils is now Congressman Gregory Meeks D Queens) But that day in August 1967, some of the players on this FB page, Raymond Reid Sr., Larry Clark, Gregory Anderson and Eddie Ingram, behind the littlest player on the team, Ronnie Murphy, pulled off the improbable. After losing every game to the Young Devils, in the Championship game, the #1 seed Young Devils faces the 3rd place South Harlem Reds., for the Championship.

. Final score South Harlem Reds 9 East Harlem Young Devils1...Ronnie Murphy was the winning pitcher, shutting down their high-powered attack. Ronnie Murphy also hit a home run and was named Championship game MVP.

The Bronx Tigers youth Football Team against the Undefeated underscored on Kiwanis Chiefs.

The Kiwanis Chiefs. Kiwanis were undefeated, underscored on. The year before, I had taken two players Ronnie Murphy and Raymond Reid, two of my Cathedral Reds baseball players, to play for the Bronx Bobcats. The Bobcats were a 12u 90lb weight limit youth football team. When you "aged out" or were too heavy to play for Bobcats, you moved up to the Bronx Tiger. The Bronx Tigers were a 13u 115lb weight limit youth football team. I had played for the Bronx Tigers.

The 1st time Coach Krupnickof the Bobcats saw Raymond Reid run, he said, "he is my starting running back". Raymond Reid did not disappoint. In the 1st quarter of the 1st game of organized football, he played. Raymond Reid ran 75 yards for a touchdown.

. After a spectacular year in which he starred for the Bobcats and made a name for himself in the Bronx/Westchester Youth

Football League, Raymond, along with Ronnie Murphy, who played fullback and mostly blocked, moved up to play for the Bronx Tigers. The Bronx Tigers were experienced and well-coached. The Bronx Tigers, unlike other youth Football teams, only had a handful of plays. The Tigers, under Coach Desmond and Coach Hadjusak, focused on execution. There were no fancy plays or deception other than a double reverse.

The Bronx Tigers were 7-0, and the game of the year, a game that a local newspaper said was between 2 of the best 13u teams on the East Coast, was coming up. The undefeated Bronx Tigers against not only undefeated Kiwanis Chiefs but unscored Kiwanis Chiefs. The Chiefs had won every game via a shutout.

This monumental game featuring a Westchester Team vs a Bronx Team was held in Van Cortland Stadium in the Riverdale section of the Bronx. Van Cortland was packed with all of Westchester, as the entire community must have come down. Two of the best teams on the East Coast were set to do battle.

The Chiefs got the ball 1st. They marched down the field with precision and power. The Tigers seemed to be no match for the Chiefs. The Chiefs lead 6-0. Now the Tigers had the ball. They gave it to their star running back, Raymond Reid, on a sweep. The Chiefs were ready, as they had heard of Raymond Reid #24, the Tigers' #1 offensive threat. The Tigers ran a sweep to the right. The Chiefs were ready. The Chiefs knocked the shit out of Raymond Reid. He fumbled the ball. He came off the field crying.

The Chiefs were celebrating like they had won the Super Bowl. They had neutralized and demoralized the Bronx Tigers' #1 weapon, or so they thought. It looked like it was going to be another Kiwanis blowout, as written later in the newspaper. I spoke to Raymond Reid as he came off the field crying. I told him to put that behind him.

The Tigers defense held and the Bronx Tigers got the ball back. You had to be there. Raymond Reid turned tears into touchdowns. It looked like a man against boys. Raymond Reid scored four touchdowns. Final score: Bronx Tigers 26, Kiwanis Chiefs 6. It was like the Atlanta Falcons versus the New England Patriots in the Super Bowl. Atlanta had what looked like an insurmountable lead. I always told my teams, "They do not give out trophies at halftime." Why did the Kiwanis Chiefs do all that celebrating? Always respect your opponent. If you beat them, beat them with class...Get used to winning, not like it is a surprise or something you do now and then. I remember I told Raymond, put that behind you and let's play. You had to be there.

Like with the tears of Raymond Reid, I always tell my players to let adversity motivate you…

We went to Cooperstown Baseball World in 2000 as the

guest of Eddie Einhorn, one of the owners of the Chicago White Sox. Debbie Sirianni ran the Camp/Tournament. Without their support, our kids could not have afforded to go there. All I asked for was a payment plan. A plan that I would personally guarantee if we fell short. We were going to wash cars, sell raffle tickets, candy what, ever we had to do to get there. These kids are from the same neighborhood where I was born and raised. Many were raised in single-parent households, as I had been. Many are without the financial resources to go on a trip like this. 8 games of baseball a week out of the city. Priceless. We also were going to the Baseball Hall of Fame in Cooperstown...

Some in the community, including some of my coaches, said we were going to get beat badly. One said we were going to get embarrassed. They wanted to push my current players aside. Players who had been there since the start. They wanted to go out and recruit the best players from Harlem and the Bronx so we could go up there and win. **Yet, I knew we had already won. The trip was never about baseball.** I knew were not being invited because we were some powerhouse team. I knew we had to take our kids. The mission, as instructed to me by God, could only be completed if we took our kids. The kids that we worked hard out in the sun. The kids we made do push-ups or run laps when the made mental and physical errors. The kids who had been dominated and humiliated in April by a future MLB pitcher who stood 6'1" at the age of 12. A team that took ass whooping after as whooping from some of the best 12u teams in New York City. But we got better and better, and we became competitive.

We went to Cooperstown Baseball World with our kids. This army we had trained this army that was hungry. We competed in Cooperstown. We won some and lost some. In Cooperstown, we lost to two of the best 12u teams you could find, but we were competitive. This made us better. We were seeded in the middle of the pack with our... .500 record. We also talked about team baseball. I used a trick question "How many base hits can a team get in an inning without scoring a run. The answer is 6. (Most people can get to 5 but cannot how to get the 6th hit without scoring a run.) When the kids would not follow the ball from the pitcher's hand to the bat, I made the whole team do push-ups. Why?, to subconsciously let the batter know he was not following the ball from the pitcher's hand to his bat? Some laughed, but we got better. I say boys because we had no girls at that time. Another story, another time.

The other major lesson that came out of this trip was about white people. My kids learned that white people were not all one and the same. They cover a vast socioeconomic range. The love between the South Harlem Reds and the white team from Maryland was special. The kids hung out together, ate together, laughed together and, at the end, gave their caps to the kids from Maryland. See, these were the kids of truck drivers, factory workers, and everyday working folks. The white team from Connecticut was another story. They never associated with the other teams and kept their distance from the South Harlem Reds. In my opinion, I think they thought they were better than both the South Harlem Reds and the Maryland team.

As God would have it, we were scheduled to play the Connecticut team in the play-off round.

They had an 8-4 lead going into the bottom of the last inning, but remember the day before, we concentrated on every conceivable way to get on base. The trick question gave them a framework, along with my signature line, that "If you do what I tell you to do, we will win this game." Do not try to be the hero. Just get on base and pass it to the next batter. Troy Andrews, who 6 years later would be scouted by several major League teams, was the leader and Captain. As with many youth teams, he was both the best pitcher and hitter. He was 12, but most of the team was 10 and 11-year-olds. They looked up to him. He had made the last out the inning before. He went off on his teammates. He put them down. The kids did all the things we had discussed the day before. All the ways to get on base. We took pitches, we were patient. Troy watched. Eventually, we got the bases loaded. We had scored 3 runs. The score was now 8-7. The Connecticut team called in their flame-throwing Ace, who was playing Center field. Two outs, the bases loaded. Travis Brady, the 9th batter of the inning, our #3 hitter as the #4 hitter, the clean up hitter in baseball vernacular Troy Andrews had made the last out the inning before. Travis Brady, was on deck hitter watching him warm up. Travis, with that bubbling "Milk Shake" smile, looked me straight in the eye and winked.

You had to be there. 1st pitch fastball outside corner. As Travis was taught to hit where it is pitched. He hit the outside pitch a line drive over 2nd base. I remember his smile to this day..he said he wrote a paper in High School about it. Brandon Milliner was in that game, Willie "Pancake" Parker, Phillip Shands, and more on our FaceBook page.

Now, maybe you understand the high I am on because it brought back so many memories of snatching victory from defeat. I remember the look on Troy Andrews face. He was crying in disbelief. The kids he had put down that he had gone off on delivered. They won it for Troy. What Troy did not see, I saw. His leadership, his tenacity, and his intense will to win had rubbed off. He had as much to do with that last inning as anyone, even though he did not bat. We went home ready for OLS Championship game versus the Mets.

The OLS Mets, who had embarrassed humiliated us, “mercy ruled us “on our home field in April, now have to face us in August for the Championship. The rest is History. Not only did we win the OLS Championship in 2000, but for 3 more years. Back to back to back to back. The South Harlem Reds!

Please share, and if you know anyone who was a participant in any of these games, please share on their page...there are many, many more. Coach Thomas Lowell says the Championship over OLS a few years later, in the 16U division when we fell behind 3-0, and they started celebrating, is his favorite. What is Yours?

.

Your Attitude Determines Your Altitude

Attitude determines your altitude. I learned that at Xerox. Listening to Rev Ike, he preached and taught a similar ideology. Your oppressor told you he was a pimp selling $5.00 prayer cloths. You listened to your oppressor and tuned Rev Ike out. The same oppressor, however, makes sure you know those marketing $10.00 made-in-China sneakers for $300.00.

Many do not have jobs and live in raggedy housing. Many will lie, cheat and steal, as well as sell poison to their own people to get the sneakers and other trinkets of deception so as to keep you enslaved. Who needs chains when one is self-enslaved?

I guess you have to have a stoop to sit on to show those sneakers off! A stoop that you call your turf but do not own. Let that sink in.

Economic Oppression and Modern-Day Slavery

Too Deep, so pass it by!

Why are the Black Masses in the conditions we are in? Why are Black so-called leaders begging for social programs? The Asians are not begging! They get results!

The Honorable Elijah Muhammad said, "The black man will never be respected until he does for himself." So-called "Black Leaders" are hand-picked by the oppressor.

This process maintains the status quo. We suffer in a system formulated on the economic theories of John Maynard Keynes. Keynesian economic theory dictates that a segment of the population be non-producing consumers. This balances the economy so the rich get richer, and the poor never revolt.

As long as the leaders in the black community keep chasing social programs from WIC to Section 8, the conditions in our community will not improve. Remember, the one who feeds you has the power to starve you. No social programs are not the answer. What I want is our piece of the rock earned over 400 years of blood, sweat and tears. Then, in the spirit of the Honorable Elijah Muhammad, we will only make babies when we can provide food, clothing and shelter and not depend on the oppressor to provide it!

May peace be unto you!

Thoughts and Reflections

Honesty of an Albuquerque Panhandler!

A guy panhandling at traffic light in Albuquerque! I asked why and what circumstances caused him to be on the street begging. He pondered, pondered & said, "I'm LAZY."

Praying with My Mother

Remembering my Mother having me pray with her as a very young boy, side by side on our knees, reminds me how BLESSED I am!

Rhetoric versus Actions

It is not what we say or do when the cameras are on but what we do at the moment of Truth when no one is watching and only God hears us! May Peace Be with You!

NBA Team Getting Blown out in the Playoffs

Desperate times call for desperate measures. I am just a playground Coach, but getting beat by almost Fiddy! We are going Full Court Man to Man, Box &1, triangle & 2, Full Court Zone Press! I am throwing chairs, eject me!

Drug Testing to get Welfare

Florida is the first state that will require drug testing when applying for welfare (effective July 1st)! Some people are crying this is unconstitutional. How is this unconstitutional, yet it's okay that every working person had to pass a drug test in order to support those on welfare? Re-post if you agree!!! Let's get Welfare back to the one's who NEED it, not those who just WANT it.

What is the Mission of Black Leaders?

Black Leaders need to focus on the mission. It is not about getting paid & being on TV, Black Man does not belong on our knees begging this Gument or the white man for anything!

Leadership, a Career or Calling?

Black Pols and ministers have made leadership a multi million dollar lifetime career! Asians have no "Media" leader Mission complete!!!!!

Asians get more done with no Identifiable Leader.

Please note that Asians have no publicly identified leader. The Man loves the Leadership "Black Buffer" class. Everything has to go through them. They have led the "Man to believe they control" you. Whether intentional or unintentional, they have sold us out a long time ago! The Man loves it the way it is!

No, "the Revolution will not be televised"

Gil Scott-Heron R.I.P. With all due respects, the Revolution will not be Televised because there will be too many potential soldiers playing video games.

All the messages and leaders. Few Listeners

Black people were not listening To Malcolm, so God sent Muhammad Ali, and the whole world listened, but do not ever be fooled into thinking that all Black People agreed. There were many in the Black Community who were NOT ready for a Black Man to openly challenge the system...I grew up listening to Ali, Malcolm and the Honorable Elijah Muhammad, I challenged everything from the White Jesus, The Bible, the Vietnam War, and the intentional flood of drugs into our community, and I still do. When we built the Baseball Field on 115th Street, we did so in the spirit of the Honorable Elijah Muhammad's "Do For Self." the Honorable Elijah Muhammad said the Black Man would never be free until he does to do for self:" The South Harlem Reds did for self, Some change but many still walking that welfare mentality road.

Why the masses "suffer" while some make millions

Someone asked how the elite make so much money while the masses suffer. My response............they control their access to knowledge by owning all the vehicles to distribute such. The masses deal with pettiness. For example, the masses can be duped into paying $250 for a pair of sneakers. Sneakers that cost a fraction of the selling to make. Sneakers made over seas in an economy where that gives little economic benefit to where the masses live....you do not have to steal from a man if he is fighting to give it to you. You can deceive a million people with a pair of sneakers but only rob one at a time with a gun....

The songs say females like pain!

I do not know how many, but a lot of females must like pain! They even singing about it! No wonder there are a lot of bad Boyz! Nice guys are getting left out!

My Mother Always challenged me to deliver and be somebody!

Democrats not much better than Trump

Most votes are against Trump. The Evil we know is better than the evil we do not know. The Democratic Evil vs the second Term Trump Evil ?

Absolute Power

We live in an age of POWER! Figuring out what is going on, commentating on it, and STOPPING it are entirely different things. Those in Power do not worry about you figuring it out. You are only important if you can STOP them.

At the decisive moment, absolute power will not disguise itself, it will not dodge you, and it will not hide! It will do its best to annihilate you! We are at that moment in history.

Success Brain Programming

As a Coach, I learned to program my players for success by the instruction they give their brain! If you say I cannot, the brain may not try! Tell it it is difficult! Now, we will find out what you have inside!

Will Politics solve the problems in the Black Community?

The Problems in the Black Community will never be resolved by Democrats and Republicans. We must build the Black Family and stop making babies with no economic game plan to take care of them except for WIC, section 8, SNAP, Subsidized Day Care, and Earned Income Credit.

These were never put there to help you., only to enslave you.. You do not have to listen to me. Go back and listen to Malcolm X. "The Best Slave is one who does not know he is a Slave." When I ask what someone will do about a problem, I mostly get silence. When politicians do have a solution, they have no chance of getting the legislation through unless it is loaded with patronage. . I have never been fooled by the. Democrats, and if Black America depends on the Democrats or Republicans to solve Our problems, We are headed down a road of destruction.

Renting versus Owning

The ignorance, the filth, the graffiti, the disrespectful behavior in our communities! If I had been paying rent for 40+ years, I would really be upset! As an owner, I have options, like the Jews did in Harlem. I can sell or rent it out and move on!

Less Policing?

For all those who wanted less Policing in NYC! You won! NYPD may not officially be on stand down, but I am sure the union has told Mayor DiBlasio that this is what you wanted. You got it!

More on less Policing.

Is NYPD on partial stand down in regards to all the "defund" the police chatter" NYC being taken over by the lawless! The news each morning is sad! Subways are unsafe despite what Mayor DiBlasio says! I guess everyone needs a security detail!

If you making so much money, pay my fee.

People are making fortunes with bitcoin mining, forex trading or getting grants but have time to send friend requests to strangers! For the people who want me to text someone, no calls, I ask them to pay the fee for me! Waiting!

Is it hard to find a God-fearing Man in Church?

Lady on Steve Harvey said She was having a hard time finding a Worthy Man. She said She wanted to be a God God-fearing man, and she was going to Church with no success, as there were mostly Women and the few Males were taken! Now, a lot of God God-fearing men do not go to Church or any Religious institution at all. Some may go to a Mosque or Synagogue, so she is limiting herself right there. Yet my point is do not exclusively equate God Fearing with the Formal practice of Religion. Fearing God and practicing a Religion is neither Mutually Inclusive nor Exclusive.

How to test for real power

Teaching Real Power! Who does Chuck Schumer call back 1st, the CEO of Goldman Sachs or the Chair of the? Congressional Black Caucus, OK! Which one does he wait until he goes to the office to call? What about Rev?

PhD. D. in Racism

Stores used to post signs in Boston N.I.N.A. "No Irish Need Apply".... so for those Irish who are in the White Power Movement, how fast after if we (Black People) were to leave before they snatch that "white" label and start calling you "Paddy or Mick" again.

Politicians out of Touch

Who's more out of touch? The President who says the $500/wk unemployment check has nothing to do with restaurants needing workers, or the Mayor who says the subways are safe?

The 364-day celebration of Mothers

Today is the REAL Mother's Day. The 1st of 364 of them. Celebrate this, the 1st of 364, by making your Mother proud of you, by putting no wrinkles on her face and no Grey hairs on her head. If you do this, if you pray with her on a regular basis, then you may understand why, I never did any big celebration for my Mother on the Sunday in May. While I acknowledged the holiday, I tried to love and celebrate her existence the other 364. So say Happy Mother's Day over the 1st of 364, not by a card or whatever, but by your actions. If you cannot do that over the 364 days before the next holiday, then all the gifts, dinner and money will never make her as happy as the Mother who is truly loved all 365, whether they are here or with the Lord...

The New Oppression

The new way of oppressing people, eliminate many of the incentives to better themselves. Give them enough to live off as long as they stay in their neighborhoods. I repeat, “their” neighborhoods!

Low Unemployment

Record number of High School Dropouts! When that stimulus & unemployment run out, maybe there will be no shortage of minimum-wage workers. Just sayin.’

Judgment Day

2 people of the same sex can do many things together under

man's law. We will all have to wait until Judgment Day to see what God has to say about it. Maybe you do not believe in judgment or God Day. No matter what the Supreme Court, the Pope and Politicians say. God is the only opinion that will matter. If God is cool with it, then everything is fine. Selling Heroin and Cocaine, you are a Bad Person under Man's Laws (Street Mentality may disagree). But on Judgment day, if God punishes all the Heroin and Cocaine Dealers, will the Broffmans and all the Liquor store owners be standing next to Nicky Barnes and all the Drug Dealers?

God's resources spent on Mars or on Cancer Research

All that Brain Power and Money to land on Mars! If it had been used to solve COVID or other diseases or to provide Aid, India may not be suffering! Lord, have Mercy on us!

Why should your customer service job be shipped somewhere else?

Called DEP to know why my water bill is so high...Got Home Girl with an attitude...So I told her to look at my bill and cxplain why payment goes to Newark NJ. One day, when I see their Union protesting about their call center jobs being exported overseas, am I supposed to feel sorry for them…

Got the world worrying about Trump while local politicians are shipping services out of state...Next thing you know, Rikers will be gone, and it will be cheaper to build prisons in China and Jet Blue will get the contract....to fly family over for a visit...

What got the Black Man into the current Economic condition?

Economics 101 Nothing is Free.

Scoring in the NBA versus winning

Russell Westbrook and Wilt Chamberlain are 2 of the greatest scorers and offensive talents of all of all time. Bill Russell is the Greatest winner.

In my opinion, here is why! Russell Westbrook is one of the best players with the ball in his hands. On average, a player has the ball in his hands 10% of the time, but a ball-dominant player like Westbrook has it 20%. To give it a historical perspective, the 20% of the time Chamberlain had the ball in his hands, he was superior to Bill Russell. In the other 80%, Bill Russell was superior to Chamberlain. Russell has 11 NBA titles, 2 NCAA and an Olympic Gold. To make Russell Westbrook relevant. Please note Nate. "Tiny" Archibald once averaged 34.7 and over 11 assists per game. Yet when asked to be a pure point guard with the Celtics, where he got his ring, he averaged what????. Case closed. Westbrook is one of the greatest scorers ever, but Bill Russell knew that winning was about more than scoring.

The next Harlem to be "Gentrified."

May the next "Harlem" be GENTRIFIED with Black Labor, Intellectual Capital, and finance, Not by those "Fronting" for the "White Man" to run you out! Do not be fooled because they look like you!

Selective Ancestry

Say it correctly "One of my 16 Great, Great, Great, Great Grandfathers was.... Ancestry has become. Commercialized! You cannot pick & choose the truth. Blood covers America's Land.

The Gument and White Man are destroying our Communities.

Listening to Luther's Live Version of "SuperStar"! I feel like we, as Black People, are losing political power every day...I hear all of our problems being blamed on the "Gument and White Man." Social Media has made experts out of so many. They can talk about every conspiracy, but they cannot give one solid game plan of how to stop it... I feel so frustrated!

Real Knowledge

When I did sales training at Xerox, I asked my sales trainees to read 3 books. I really recommend them to anyone making money and spending it. Any book on negotiating, Any book on selling, If you can find. it....."Winning through Intimidation" Why on selling if you are not a salesperson? Look on virtually any cover of the book "The Art of War." The quote explains why.....It starts with "If you know yourself..., I do try to share what I learned from the "WhiteMan" aka Xerox and IBM. Paraphrasing Minister Farrakhan, said your people will reject it!

Pointing the Blame for Gentrification

Did you not learn anything from the Tale of the 3 Talents in the Bible, as it pertains to Gentrification & Gument feel sorry programs? It is a sophisticated Con Game. You sat on your Talents(aka wealth) & now you want to blame someone!

What is important to you?"

Damn, "Niggas" will pay $800.00 for a phone, Two Fiddy for some sneakers", but not $35.00 for a financial calculator, a tool that will enable you to save money for the rest of their life. Self-imposed slavery of the mind.

Financial Warfare

If you and I go into a car dealer and buy the same car, I am going to most likely get a better deal than you! I have my financial calculator in my hand and all the knowledge the "White Man" taught me at Xerox, IBM and from books!

Spend your money where?

Which product does Black America spend the most on that puts the fewest Black people to work here while employing many overseas?

Trying to share knowledge

Only one person is showing interest in my financial warfare seminar. Like Louis Farrakhan said, if we could take home what we learned in Corporate America, we could almost free our people overnight...Please note Jim DiGruttila mentions he still has the financial calculator I trained him on. 30 years ago. I did Sales and Financial training at Xerox. I was paid very well. People like Jim did very well financially. Yet, when I try to give knowledge to my people for free, it is usually rejected. You keep waiting on the Gument and it's freebies. That Welfare Mentality got so many of my people stuck in a rut... By the way, it is beautiful in the desert. I will be busting the Apple soon...,

Outside the Box thinkers

The most Powerful and least listened to or virtually ignored Black Person is the one who has "Outside the box" knowledge. Knowledge takes you outside your comfort zone. There is no heroin, weed or alcohol that can medicate that feeling.

Can you give everything to everybody?

Why Bidens' speech kept me awake, everything has a price. This economy is run on Keynesian Economic Theory. Biden's proposal was like a QB looking great in practice with no stress. Biden will face a defense with players named Lobbyists, PACs, Special Interests and Political Patronage. His programs will make the poor poorer. Malcolm starts my school of thought on this. It starts with the tale of the 3 Talents in the Bible. . You must reward those who multiply their Talents . , not the ones who buried his and did nothing. I did about 10 Live videos. I have covered a lot of this in my videos. I am sure many may not understand what I said or agree with me. So let it be!

Made in America sounds really Simple. When it is written into law, it will be a few hundred-page definition. The Lobbyists and Special interests will define "Made in America." It will not match your definition.

Tim Scott and Joe Biden are both elitists who are out of touch with America! One says America is not racist, and the other tells you you can have everything in the store for free!

Greatest Economic Plan in History! If there were no lobbyists, PACs and Champagne and Lobster Dinners! Wipe the "Theory of Comparative Advantage" out of the MBA curriculum.

Why is there Wealth Inequality in America?

Wealth Inequality in America? Start with the tale of the 3. Talents in the Bible Mix in the Devil Mix in those who do nothing and think Jesus got them!

Thinking on a higher level

It is not what you say but what you do not say and the 2nd level analysis. The street meaning of Chickens coming home to roost is what comes around goes around. The comment in regards to JFK is that when Political Assassinations have been ordered and carried out by the CIA under the auspices of the President, such as Nkrumah and Lumumba, to stop Africa from being shaped into One Nation like the USA, so as its resources would not be exploited, actually came back to bite the USA in the Ass. That, along with the Co-Intell Program, was out of the box thinking for America at that time. That is why he (Malcolm) got censured. JFK was a loved Man, but now the truth about JFK is coming out.

Voter fraud, but not enough to overturn the election

I Voted in New Mexico A lot more security to ensure against fraud. In NY, they still send stuff for My Mother, despite what I do! Big time for fraud in NY I believe!

Power and Will

Power only submits to superior power. Will is the most powerful force on the Face of the earth. Will carried Gandhi & MLK to fight superior force. We are up against a NASTY ENEMY. We cannot be denied if we collectively use our will.

Master of your own ship

You are the Master of Your own ship. Being poor and broke at one time in your life is one thing. Being that way chronically, you may way to ask the Admiral what map is he/she reading or in 2021 does, the GPS have juice.

Do not ask Black People this.

If you want to get your head bit off, ask this question: "What has the Gument or White Man stopped you from doing over the past 90 days that was not the result of something you did

Make up your mind. You are going to make it!

Making it in life. I know our history and struggle as well as anyone. Even with "good" jobs, that knee is still on our necks. Focusing on today, I ask who, born in America, has no choice but to work at minimum wage. What I try to get those who believe in me or are inspired by me is to focus on what we can control.

Getting an education or skill, staying out of trouble, staying away from illegal drugs, and only using legal drugs like alcohol, marijuana and cigarettes in moderation to the extent it does not interfere with your ability to pursue life, liberty and happiness. Too many out there selling excuses to us while getting rich off the excuse selling. I know the formula that leads us to a better life. I always loved the story of a friend's father going to her Mother's job and telling her boss she was not working there anymore. He taught his kids about work and responsibility, and as a Man, he put a roof over their heads and food on the table. Those are the basic principles we have gotten away from.

Yes, a lot had been done and is being done every day to stop us. We are a better people than that! That is why my Mother stuck that finger in my face and told me I had to be twice as good as the "white boy". This is one of the lessons I grew up with. I am just trying to pass on some of that love and wisdom. If they want to listen to the excuses, listen to them. If they want to know how to make it listen to me...then too maybe I have not made it????

Liberation Math

Liberation Math! How many Blunts, Weaves, Nails done, and Nike Sneakers add up to $5,000.00? Waiting! Ask AC, my man on FaceBook, Inquiring minds want to know.

Jesus as a modern lesson on power

Those in power looked for Baby Jesus to KILL Jesus because he was a threat! They were going to slit a baby named

Jesus's throat! You all keep using Social Media for BS! Those Trump represents are dangerous.

Clean Uniforms

South Harlem Reds, why I wanted clean, fitting, simple uniforms

When you look good, you feel good

When you feel good, you are good

When you are good , you can play with anybody!

Coach, I cannot pay now for my child to go on trip

2 types of parents who ask if their child can go on a trip, and they will pay you later. The parent who, when they get the money, will pay you. Then there is the parent who never intends to pay you!

On behalf of the South Harlem Reds, I have received cards a year later from parents with the funds inside for the trip. They express sincere gratitude for allowing their child to participate. For the other group, what can I say? Maybe they thought they were getting over. How do I feel? “To whom much is given, much is required.” I understand what God Blessed me to do! I answer to God, not Man.! May Peace Be Unto You!

Patting myself on my back.

One of the Biggest Accomplishments in My Life is that at the age of 15, I took a group of kids from 115th Street and Lenox, with all the drugs, poverty, ignorance and crime and **made Them Believe They could They could be Champions!** you can smirk at, try to minimize, laugh at, or dismiss, but that is 100% Fact.

Poems

(Sistas, to let you know I understand)

Single Mothers

When age comes how, I will explain

Decisions are made of sunshine, sometimes rain

God knows I have loved as best as I can

There will be those who say where is your MAN?

I looked, I searched, I pondered and Prayed

To a higher power, my decision has stayed

By many judgments will already have been rendered

But to me, God's ultimate gift has been my way tendered

In the beauty of darkness, may a life of light prevail?

To some, it may be a sin, but God's love does not fail

While God, have you allowed me a destiny incomplete

Yet I know this is so much deeper than passion on a sheet

Was I so unrighteous in search of a mate?

Did I judge reality on a dance, clothes, car or a date?

Did I look for a doctor lawyer and confuse such with a man

Another date with spirituality, God be it may or simply can

Will the Day of Judgment be an eternity as I present my case

. God, please accept my decision of love and dedication face-to-face!

Toughest Decision

The day I have prayed for his family arrived

So sweet, so beautiful, with pretty true eyes

Do I give the father the honor of documentation?

Such a beauty of God could only be his creation

To be single not only at the moment of truth

My inner motive is will take a master sleuth

Has society put on us an unattainable goal?

What I feel is so deep, deep in the soul

We think that ideal mate must look like an Adonis

Really unimportant things by man have been put upon us

Will he love, cherish, care, provide not just lust

'to thine self be true' as Shakespeare said

To my soul, I must explain why I'm not wed

To wait for the perfect man, I may wait an eternity

Yet I have faith that God will carry me through this journey

Sistas, to let you know I understand

Poem Superficial Love

To many in college, he was what some called a nerd

ballplayer no, no popular frat no member of the herd

my roommate and her crew required 6 feet two

No way, she laughed and taunted would he do

no, he was not the greatest dancer, as the song sang

see, he had to be there Sunday when the church bells rang

too many look for a man based on superficial

then, when they are hurt, cry tears into a tissue

the day that God took a loved one from me

this friend was there for only God and I to see

I took them not seriously for they thought he was not fine

then God Almighty planted a vision understanding mine

he let me know if my essence was simply physical delight

that they would be many a day, I would cry through the night

a real man with first submit his will to God above

his true essence will be peaceful and sweet, like a dove

his marriage Vows, he will dissect and obey

You see, it will be our first and only wedding day.

Unfulfilled Superstar

The epitome of beauty, class and grace

I remember the first look at her face

tall, sweet and cool, so chocolate brown

she was the unknown superstar of the town

to her, unbeknownst, some fantasized, even a scheme

a fantasy perhaps, but what is life without a dream

to make love to her would be the ultimate delight

whether for an eternity or as Luther sang for just one night

I trust, hope and pray there is someone who worships her

Who will shower her with not just jewels, diamonds and fur

but the ultimate love that a lady of her status has earned

the type of love that comes from God is innate, not learned

May she find the love and family she is waiting to bear

some of God's precious children to be in her care

of course, ring, wedding bells, church and flowers

The planning, the rehearsal on my God, countless hours

But oh God, if destiny does not walk her down the aisle

Send a special Man to be the Father of her Children.

Sistas, What type of Man did you Pray for?

To the Sistas, did you Pray to God for a Man or a Male? Did you describe physical Characteristics like Height, Weight, Hair, Skin Color, type of Ride, Gucci Fiorucci, was being the Greatest Dancer etc important? Mmmm, maybe God God sent you what you Prayed for? And he was a Nightmare?

Or did You Pray for one who would love and respect you? Did you Pray for one who submitted his will to God and not just settle for going to church? Did you Pray for one who was Honest, Morally Correct, and Respectful of His Mother, not by gifts but by deed? Did When God sent him into your life not he not meet your Physical Dreams? Are You Happy?

About the Author

Maurice Faucette was born and raised in Harlem, a product of the Great Southern migration, with his mother hailing from Alabama and his father from Durham, NC. He grew up in the neighborhood depicted in the movie "American Gangster," with the Nation of Islam Mosque #7, led by Malcolm X and later by Louis Farrakhan, just around the corner. Malcolm X's rallies were held on his block, where he learned the teachings that emphasized the importance of Black self-sufficiency.

Maurice's father left the family, and he was raised by his mother in a Harlem tenement building with his five siblings. Despite facing challenges, his mother worked three jobs instead of relying on welfare. Maurice was an exceptional student in his early years but lost interest in school around the 7th grade. Although he loved sports and started coaching at the age of 14, his experience in a predominantly white school in the Bronx led to a dislike for education. It wasn't until his sophomore year at NCCU that Maurice gained a new perspective on education, as outlined by Dr. Jawanza Kunjufu's book, "Countering the Conspiracy to Destroy Black Boys."

Maurice faced a turning point when he visited his hospitalized mother during semester probation. Responsible for his 14-year-old sister and 9-year-old brother, he realized the importance of taking care of his family. Despite struggles, Maurice graduated with over a 3.0 GPA in Business. Working with Lindsey Merritt in the NCCU Placement Office, he received multiple job offers and full-paid graduate school opportunities but chose to return to Harlem to support his mother. Working at Xerox Corp, Maurice fulfilled his childhood dreams by providing for his family and securing a new home for them in the North Bronx.

Over the years, Maurice has been actively involved in the community, serving as CEO and board member of the West Harlem Community Organization, focusing on bringing affordable housing to Harlem. He collaborated with Rev. Calvin O. Butts III, Pastor of Abyssinian Baptist Church, in "New Voices for Harlem," addressing political issues in the community. At the age of 14, Maurice founded the South Harlem Reds Baseball Program, a self-help initiative that has mentored countless inner-city youth. Additionally, he was the President of the People's Forum for Change Political Club and a member of C.A.E.E. (Community Advocates for Educational Excellence), dedicated to improving education in Harlem. Maurice has made appearances on Tony Brown's Journal and Court Television.

A graduate of North Carolina Central University with a B.S.C. in Business and a minor in Mathematics, Maurice also attended Lehman College for education and Fordham University's Graduate School of Business. His career in sales, mainly at Xerox

Corp, saw him rise to the position of Sales Manager, and he served three times as President of MAME, the Black Employees Association at Xerox.

Media Appearances

Tony Brown's journal "Is Self Help Too Much Work"

- Speech to NY Bar Association on Diversity. Court Television
- Night Line "Million Man March" Interviewed at Penn Station
- Good Day NY TV with Dick Oliver South Harlem Reds Baseball Program
- News 12 News clips and commentary
- Growing with Grace Cable TV interview (2)
- Several newspaper articles on the South Harlem Reds, most prominent "Sad Day for the Field of Dreams" Jim Dyer NY Daily News April 15, 1997 (Jackie Robinson 50th Anniversary of breaking the color barrier)

Maurice G Faucette

southharlemsport@aol.com

MGFHarlemBronx (YouTube Channel)

718-881-1738

His dynamic speaking style has bought hope to many who hear his message. He inspires youth when he tells them how he bought his Mother a brand new home 5 years after graduating college after growing up in a cold water rat infested slum building.

Made in the USA
Middletown, DE
25 October 2024